WHAT IF IT HURTS

shirl rickman

WHAT IF IT HURTS

DEDICATION

This story created a new confidence in me. One that I'm embracing and trying to spread to all areas of my life. I didn't get here alone though. First, I would like to send so much love to my husband, Ryan, who never allows me to give up. He pushes me to take time for myself and for my creativity. His pride in me is uplifting and the main ingredient in my confidence to keep pushing forward.

Thank you to my reader group, Rickman Readers, for sticking by me. To Colette Kishbaugh for keeping it all going.

I would also like to thank my friend Sara Ney, who shared some new secrets to keeping on track and sticking to goals. It made a huge difference in my ability to complete this story on time. Thank you to my childhood pal, Erin Althaus of Purple is Proofreading for once again stepping in and being a part of my team to get this book out. Another huge thank you goes out to Chelle Northcutt for being thorough and honest with your feedback. I joke that you're scary but it's in the best way. I choose your help because I know you want to help me put out the best story I can for my readers and that is what is most important to me. And finally, thank you to Stacy Garcia for giving Maddie and Ryder's story such a beautiful cover. And to Alyssa Garcia finishing it all off with the perfect look inside.

Writing a book takes a village and I love all the people in mine.

CHAPTER 1

Maddie

I'm an imperfect person. I know it. I feel it. Undeniably, others know it too. I'm okay with that fact. No one is perfect.

This is the only thing I know about myself, and I'm unsure how to figure life out.

I blink back, the sleep threatening to take over as these thoughts whirl through my head along this lonely California highway.

I'm trying to convince myself I'm not running away from my past but sprinting full speed ahead toward my future. I mean, that's what I told my mama when she cried, holding me tightly against her chest while she asked me why I was leaving her. My family. My friends. The place I call home. My mind drifts back to just before I began this journey.

I don't know Mama. I just…I feel like there is something there I need to find. The words I whispered to her as tears filled my eyes echo through my mind. She just squeezed tighter and then let me go. I felt the breath she released as I waited for the words she would use to convince me I was making a mistake. It was her usual approach to anything I did that she disagreed with, which, as much as I tried to please her and my Daddy, seemed to happen often. Except, this time was different. The exhale of air that left her was all that came as she pushed back from me one last time. I could see it in her eyes—she was finally letting her baby grow up.

Ironically, I wanted to scream and throw myself back into her arms. Beg her to ask me not to go. I wanted to be convinced for the first time in all my twenty-three years I didn't know what a huge mistake I was making. But instead, I swallowed the knot in my throat, stepped back, and turned to my dad. My dad…Daddy…tears in his eyes that would never fall; he only looked at me and gave me that smile I loved so much. The one that said he loved me and always would. The smile that told me I was safe when I felt scared and the expression that said I'd always be perfect enough for him. I hugged them both one last time and got in my Honda Civic, stuffed to the roof with everything I owned.

Now, I'm seventeen hours into my journey and in dire need of a pit stop. I've nearly done the impossible. I haven't stopped for more than a bathroom break, a snack, and gas. I can't get there fast enough. Cambria. A place I visited one summer as a kid with my grandparents. Which takes me back to the fact that I'm not running. I'm not, although I've spent the entire trip trying to persuade myself of that. I know exactly what I'm doing, and it has nothing to do with running away from lost hopes, dreams, and a love that consumed every fiber of my being. No, he had nothing to do with it. Regardless of why, I realize I need to find a place to stop.

The thump of the reflectors lining the side of the road breaks me from my thoughts and warns me to bring my eyes and the tires back on the road. I notice the bright light of a motel sign shining like a beacon in the night, calling to the drivers seeking sanctuary from the barren desert night. As I pull into the parking lot, I debate if I will park beneath one of the fluorescent parking lot lights or rent a room for the night. Why spend the hundred and fifty dollars for less than a night's sleep? I opt for curling up in the driver's seat with my head and pillow propped against the window. I look at the parking lot and take in my surroundings. If I stay in a well-lit area, no one should bother me…I hope.

Closing my eyes, I try to allow the sleep my body desperately needs to take over. While my eyes remain shut, my mind continues to race through my past. The memories of my choices over the last few years are clouded with heartache, disappointment, and poor decisions. I lost myself completely, and the worst part is that I feel as if the real me has been on the outside looking in on someone else's life. All because I gave my heart away when I was just fourteen years old and never realized the consequence of what that actually meant.

A slight smile touches my lips in my sleepy haze as the tune of my favorite '90s music icon, Eminem, plays in my mind. Sleep finally begins to take over, and my last thought is, will the real Madelyn Jennings please stand up?

CHAPTER 2

Maddie

My eyes bounce from the check engine light that came on about five miles back to the mileage marker sign of the town I'm approaching now. Village of Cambria. Population: 5,000. Relief floods me, knowing I have only about two miles to reach the bed and breakfast I will live and work in.

I continue to roll along to my destination, feeling anxious as my nerves and excitement intermingle deep in my belly.

The little Village of Cambria is just as quaint as I remember. Small boutiques, cafés, bakeries, and restaurants line the main street in hopes of attracting tourists. I even see a few antique shops sprinkled in between. I love it. It all seems so hopeful for some reason, and that is precisely what I'm looking for right now.

My GPS indicates my turn onto Moonstone Beach Drive is coming up.

I turn along the street lined with trees and full of curb appeal. It's so perfect and pretty—the bright, vibrant greens from the large trees that sprawl along the road and the pinks and yellows from the blooming flowers.

I finally see the wooden sign standing in a small clearing beside the driveway. "Moonstone Bed and Breakfast" is painted in bright white and trimmed in a soft yellow. Slowly, I pull into the drive and continue until I stop in front of the enormous Craftsman-style home with a wraparound porch. It's painted the same soft yellow as the sign, but the trim is a deep green instead of white.

Tears begin to slip from the corners of my eyes—exhaustion, relief, and happiness. A small sigh escapes as I rest my head on the steering wheel. There are so many unknowns about moving my life here, but the hope I felt as I drove into town along the central street moments ago, I feel here now.

A tap on the window startles me from my thoughts, and I let out a yelp.

Looking out my driver-side window, I see a smiling elderly couple standing outside my car with warm smiles spread across their faces. Henry and Evelyn Evans. They look just the same as I remember. It's like they haven't changed in the thirteen years since I was here. I give them both an embarrassed smile and open my door to step out.

"Hello, we're so sorry we took you by surprise," Evelyn says in a gentle, kind voice.

Henry laughs a gruff sort of laugh. "Not our intention," he agrees.

I smile. "No worries, I'm naturally jumpy."

Evelyn steps forward first to embrace me. "You must be Madelyn," she says, pulling me into a hug that feels like my own grandmother's comforting embrace. Henry grins behind her, and when she pulls back, he turns in for his turn. I obviously reciprocate the gesture willingly.

"Yes, and you're Mr. and Mrs. Evans," I respond. "You both look as I remember."

Henry waves away my statement. "Not a chance, young lady; it's been thirteen years." Then, once again, he lets out a strong whoop. At that moment, I realized I would really like Henry Evans. He seems to be a person who enjoys living with humor and takes life in stride—something I need to do more of.

Evelyn grins, "I must agree with Henry, but it's kind of you. Also, please call us Henry and Evelyn. There are no formalities here. You're family." She pauses before continuing, "Charles and Addie have shown us pictures and written letters, regaling all the details of your life, so it's like we know you. You've grown into such a beautiful young lady, so when they told us you wanted an adventure in California and were hoping you might find your place here, it felt right for you to stay in the back cottage and work here with us. We need the help, so it is impeccable timing." Henry nods beside his wife.

A wide smile plays across my features, and I move in to hug Evelyn once more.

"Thank you both so much. It means so much, and I promise I won't be a burden while I'm here. My major in college was hospitality, so this is a perfect opportunity for me," I assure them both.

"And it works for us as well, "Evelyn says.

"Well, now that we've all agreed having Madelyn here will have a positive impact on us all, let's get her things unloaded so she can get settled into the cottage," Henry says.

"It's Maddie," I tell them both. "Please call me Maddie. It's what my family calls me."

Evelyn reaches for my hand, "Okay, Maddie. Let's start by having you move your car around to the back, closer to the cottage and where we park."

"Speaking of driving, I know this old girl can make it to the back, but I'll need to find a mechanic tomorrow to look at her. My check engine light came on nearly eight miles back," I explain.

Henry pats my shoulder, "No problem. We know a great mechanic."

"Great," I say with some relief.

"Just pull around that way," Henry tells me as he points to the left of the house. "We will meet you back there so I can help you carry your things inside."

I nod as I slide back into the driver's seat of my Honda and start the engine. The old girl is sounding a bit under the weather, for sure. I hope this mechanic knows what he's doing, and it won't cost my entire savings to get her fixed.

Henry and Evelyn walk across the lawn and around the side of the main house, so I follow along on the driveway in the same direction. Pulling my car around the side, I see my new home nestled back about a hundred yards behind the main house. It's a miniature version, painted the same color and just as welcoming. The only difference is its size and the fact the porch only covers the front of the home. It's incredible, and I can't help the wide grin on my face.

I stop the car in the drive just next to the cottage and get out, taking in my surroundings. I can't take my eyes off my new home.

"So, what do you think?" Henry asks.

"It's more than I could've hoped for," I tell them.

Clasping her hands together, Evelyn says, "Oh, we're thrilled to hear that, Maddie."

"Let's unload your things so you can settle in and get some rest. It will be dark soon," Henry says.

Luckily, I only brought what would fit in my car—a few boxes of books and knick-knacks from home. My mama gave me my clothes, computer, and a unique stained-glass lamp. It took us all of fifteen minutes to get everything into the house, which is just as adorable on the inside as it is on the outside.

"Dinner will be on the table in an hour, so I hope you're hungry and will join us," Evelyn tells me.

They're standing in the doorway, obviously trying to give me space.

"Sure, I would like to shower first, and then I'll head up."

"Fine, see you soon," Evelyn says, Henry already walking away. "And Maddie, we're so happy to have you here with us. We hope you find what you're looking for here."

I smile at them. "Thank you." Slowly spinning around, I take in the open-spaced room. "I have a feeling I will," I say, but when I turn to face the doorway again, Evelyn has already caught up with Henry, and they're walking hand in hand across the backyard.

Closing the door, I turn to face the room and lean back with a loud, thankful sigh.

"Home," I whisper out loud.

There it is again, that feeling of hope. Except this time, it feels like it's transforming into something more tangible than just a feeling.

• • •

A couple of hours later, I'm back in my cottage alone. Dinner was delicious, and I'm happily stuffed to the gills. There was even a fresh fruit cobbler for dessert. Evelyn is a fantastic cook, and I can see what a treat it is for any guest to stay here. Comfort and quality. It makes me even more excited to work here.

I'm exhausted, but I can only think about unpacking my things.

My mama would love this place. I snapped a few pictures before heading to dinner and texted them to my parents. The photos don't do justice to just how incredible this place is. There's also a feeling I get just standing in this room. Mama and I planned to talk the next day since it was getting late there. I'm going to have to get used to this two-hour time difference.

I opened my boxes of books and began to unload them onto the antique wooden bookshelf in the living area. The room is open, and I imagine it's bright during the day with the crisp white walls and the number of windows that will allow plenty of sunlight in. The kitchen has abundant counter space and cabinets for being on the smaller side.

One of the many perks of living here is that the home is furnished and filled with everything I need.

Evelyn told us there were plenty of clean sheets and blankets for the bed. They told me I could do whatever I wanted to make this house my home. They're generous and kind and welcoming—everything I could wish.

I think of the home I left and my drive here. I think of my past and what I want for my future. All of these things run through my head as I unpack everything I brought from my past into my present.

By the time I finish and look at the clock, it's eleven thirty, and the only thing I can think of now is my first full night's sleep in a bed in days. After I brush my teeth and wash my face, I throw back the covers of my new bed in my new room and crawl beneath them. Pulling the comforter around me, I say a short prayer and close my eyes.

It doesn't take long before the exhaustion of starting this new chapter in my life takes over.

CHAPTER 3

Maddie

My eyes blink open, and for a passing minute, my sleepy, foggy brain doesn't remember where I am. Cambria. A tiny smile spreads across my face. Rubbing the sleep from my eyes, I roll onto my back and stare at the ceiling. I think about how good it feels to be here. In this room. In this home. My home.

It feels good to think of this place as home.

Sunlight peeks through the blinds covering the window. It's beautiful and peaceful. As soon as the thought crosses my mind, I hear a loud banging outside my window. One would have been fine, but the sound blasts again.

What in the hell is that?

I jump out of bed and peer through the blinds. Someone is in my car. I can't see who it is, but I can tell it isn't Henry. Knocking on the window, I start yelling, "Excuse me, what are you doing in my car?" The person doesn't even look my way; they keep doing whatever they do. Great, am

I being robbed on my second day here? I don't care if I'm only wearing tiny sleep shorts and a small, cropped band T-shirt; I head straight for the front door.

Swinging the door open, I rush around the porch to the side of the cottage where my car is parked, hollering again before I even reach the car, "Excuse me! Can I help you with something?" I still can't see who it is because now my hood is up and blocking my view of the culprit. I stop dead in my tracks as the mystery intruder comes around the front of my car into view.

He's tall and lean. Dark hair, almost black, worn long on the top. I can still see the sharp edges of his facial features beneath the scruff covering his jawline. When his pale green eyes lock with mine, I suck in a quick breath. This stranger can't be described as anything other than breathtaking. I've lost the fire behind my emotions.

One corner of his mouth tips up as he stares back at me, wiping his hands clean.

The smirk only adds to his appeal, but the gleam in his eye rubs me the wrong way for some reason, reigniting my initial annoyance at a stranger messing with my car without my knowledge.

Finally finding my voice, I square my shoulders and place my hands on my hips in a confident stance. I push aside the way my body feels, just looking at this guy I don't even know.

"Pardon my French, but who the hell are you?" I don't know what I said that he found so funny, but it must be something because he lets out a loud, boisterous howl.

"What's so funny?" I ask indignantly.

Shaking his head, he steps toward me, and I instinctively step back. He takes another step toward me, reaching his hand out. "I'm Ryder. Ryder Evans. Henry and Evelyn are my grandparents. You must be Madelyn Jennings." I look down at his hand and push my own out to him. "Uh...yes, I'm Maddie." He envelopes my hand in his, holding it gently, and I glance up into those mesmerizing eyes. This was the moment I realized where I'd seen this color before; they were the same color as Evelyn's eyes. It just looks different on...Ryder. Suddenly, we release each other's hand. Ryder continues, "My grandpa asked if I would come take a look at your car since I'm a mechanic."

I sigh in regret. I quickly apologize for reacting before understanding what is going on. "I'm sorry. Being in a new place, and then I heard a loud noise coming from out here and was startled," I tell him.

"No worries, but uh..." he replies, waving his hand up and down in my direction before continuing, "I think I know what's wrong and want to go over that with you, but I can wait while you go change." Glancing down at myself, I cringe. I'm showing more of myself than I usually would to a stranger. "Uh, yeah. I'll be right back," I say, returning toward the cottage.

As I walk away, I glance back and find Ryder with his head back under the hood of my car. I guess I was the only one affected by our encounter.

Ryder

Squeezing the bridge of my nose between my fingers, I

work on gaining my composure. It isn't often I'm taken off guard, but just one look at my grandparent's new boarder and employee has me tripped up a bit.

As soon as I caught sight of those long, toned, tan legs and flat abdomen, I felt a little off balance—something I don't like to feel very much. I've seen plenty of girls come and go through this town with similar physiques, so why the reaction? I guess I just wasn't expecting the Madelyn Jennings that Gramps and Gram have been going about for weeks to look the way she does.

"So, did you figure things out yet, Ry?" My grandpa pops up from around the side of the car. Man, he is stealthy for someone his age.

"Well, I'm certain it's just a couple of bad spark plugs, which is good news because it's an easy fix," I tell him without missing a beat.

"Did I hear you say easy fix?" her timid, sweet voice says from behind me. This reaction is a complete change from the fiery woman who charged around the corner of the house at me minutes ago. When I turned around, Maddie was looking at me expectantly. "Sorry, I just thought I heard you say …"

Interrupting her, I say, "No need to apologize; I believe it's something easy. I'm one hundred percent positive it's just some bad spark plugs. I can head into the shop, then stop back by later and install them here. Do you need your car?"

Pushing a strand of loose, auburn hair behind her ear, Maddie smiles, "Nope, I think I can just walk to work today." Grandpa chuckles in his usual way. "Good morning,

15

Henry," she says, still grinning from ear to ear. She directs her attention back to me. "Look, I want to apologize again for acting like a crazy person a few minutes ago, like I said, new place and all. I truly appreciate you doing this for me when you don't even know me."

"I said don't worry about it, so please don't worry about it," I tell her, keeping my voice neutral and short.

I see her flinch slightly, but I don't apologize.

"I missed some excitement this morning already?" Grandpa asks.

Maddie shrugs, "I may have come out guns a blazing and a bit unnecessarily concerned for my car." Her cheeks flush a light rose color, and she can't seem to look me in the eyes.

"Nah, I should've waited until she was up before I started banging around out here," I say. "Anyway, I better be on my way. I'll be back after work today," I tell them as I head toward my truck.

"See you later, son. Should I tell your Gram you'll join us for dinner tonight?" Grandpa asks just as I'm sliding behind the steering wheel.

Closing the door, I lean out the open window. "Gramps, we both know I don't have a choice in that matter, so I'm not certain why you're asking." Grandad chortles, and I give him a knowing smile.

Maddie stands silently next to Grandpa with her lips turned up in a wide grin. Her eyes lock with mine when I look in her direction, and she says, "Thank you again, Ryder."

I give her a nod before backing down the driveway.

Glancing back into the rear-view mirror, I see Grandpa telling Maddie something animated because his hands are flying around, and she is holding her middle and laughing like she's never heard anything funnier. I can only imagine what he's telling her.

I find myself smiling, too, as I turn out of the drive and head into work. Something new is in the air, and I'm not sure I'm comfortable with it yet.

CHAPTER 4

Maddie

Work today consisted of a delicious, hot breakfast and a tour of the rooms and the property with a sprinkle of jokes in between. Evelyn and Henry insisted I have one more day of rest since the check-out and check-in day for the current and future guests is tomorrow.

"Please let us know if you need anything," Evelyn tells me as I return to my cottage. She stands in the doorway with the screen door pushed open.

"I will, but I think I have everything I need for now. Thank you so much for this opportunity," I reply, walking down the path.

"It's our pleasure." She gives me a sweet smile.

There is a gentle kindness in her look. One that makes me feel comforted, and I'm thankful for that. Uprooting my entire life and leaving behind every hope and dream I had for as long as I can remember hasn't been easy. Being here with her and Henry will allow me to explore ways to find whatever God has intended for me.

As Mama would say, I need to let go and let God. And moving to Cambria was the first step in letting go.

When I reach the doorway of my new home, I turn and look out over the expanse of the yard. So many trees and bright green grass were covering the ground before me. Vividly colored flowers and plants are everywhere. A wide grin spreads across my face because it all just seems hopeful, and that's a feeling I've been missing for a while.

Startled from my thoughts by the ring of my phone, I pull it from my pocket and glance down at the screen. An old picture of me and Mama; I smile and swipe to answer.

"Mama," I say into the phone with a smile.

"Hi, baby girl," she says in her usual way. "How's your first official day in California?"

"Well, it's only ten o'clock in the morning here, so the day is only starting, but I can say it's off to a great start," I tell her.

She chuckles, "Dang, the time difference. I'm going to have a hard time getting used to it."

Chuckling, I say, "Me, too. Especially with my sleep schedule."

Walking into my living room, I plop down on the sofa.

"Mama, you wouldn't believe this place. It's exactly as I remember it from my visit here with Mamaw and Papaw, but also so different. It's amazing what you miss when you're a little kid."

Mama snorts. I love that sound and man; it makes me miss her.

"Baby girl, it's just a different view, or should I say a different lens as you age," she tells me.

"Yeah, I'm sure seeing life through a different lens these days. It makes me wonder why it took me so long to reach this clarity." I sigh into the phone, and silence passes between us for a moment. It's like she's giving me a little time to mourn my loss of naivety. Aren't those what early life choices are like for some of us? Always seeing the good, we forget that sometimes we need to make a few choices with our heads and not the desires of our hearts.

"Maddie. Listen to me; there is a reason someone came up with the saying, 'Looking through rose-colored glasses,' but no one said it's always a bad thing. Sometimes, we must make choices that lift us instead of keeping us down. Life is a constant wheel of lessons, full of ups and downs, twists and turns, and it's all about keeping true to yourself. You've spent the better part of your life making choices based on other people's happiness and what you think everyone thinks you should do instead of looking at what will make you happy. This is your time, baby. And I couldn't be prouder of you."

"Thanks, Mama. But what if this was a mistake?" I ask.

"What if it isn't?" she responds.

"Mama, I hope I'm as wise as you one day," I tell her. One of the things I've been working on is telling my parents how grateful I am for them and how incredibly wonderful parents they are to me.

"You will be wiser because you're already making braver choices than I ever have in my life," Mama says in response. "Well, I better let you get on with your day, and I need to get on with mine."

"Tell Daddy hello, and I love him."

"Sure will. Bye, baby."

"Bye, Mama."

The phone clicks on the other end of the line, ending the call. I think about her last statement about me making brave choices. Is that what this is? Is it a bold choice to move halfway across the country to escape my past? Or is it about perspective? Should the real question be, is it a brave choice to move halfway across the country to find myself? My mind hasn't made up its decision on that answer just yet.

• • •

Walking through the tiny town, I take in my surroundings. It's small yet busy. When I drove into town yesterday, I noticed all the little shops calling to each tourist walking by them. Now I get to take it all in. There is something for everyone. Antique lovers and book lovers. Vintage clothing patrons and cute boutique shoppers. Coffee shops and cafes with ice cream counters. This town really does have everything, but it's managed to keep its quaint charm.

A slight breeze blows through the streets, carrying the scent of the ocean.

I inhale a deep breath and let out a satisfied sigh. I love the way it smells and the feeling it gives me.

Ahead of me, I spot the local mechanic shop at the end of the main street. It's a brick building garage, and standing just outside is Ryder Evans, a smile spread across his face as he chats with a tiny blonde twirling her hair between her fingers. She's wearing a low-cut top and trendy booty shorts. She's gorgeous. A girlfriend? She definitely matches him in the looks department. It hits me as I watch them interact—his eyes never leave her face. I can't help but focus on that thought. Any other guy I know would let his gaze drop to all the bare skin she's offering to admire. But not Ryder. I can't help but stare at them.

It's just my luck that the one time he decides to look away, he doesn't look at the blonde's body but instead directly at me. His lips turn up at the corners.

Knowing I've been caught staring, I wave my hand in a quick hello and dart into the coffee shop.

When I peek out the window, I catch a glimpse of him and notice the blonde is now looking in the same direction he is. She says something, and shaking his head, Ryder turns his attention back to her.

I watch a minute longer until I hear a loud, kind voice call from behind me. "Welcome! Can I get you anything?"

Shifting my thoughts to the greeting, I turn and find a pretty young brunette grinning from behind the counter. "Uh, yeah…hello, I definitely want something, but I'm unsure what you have here."

"Well, that's what I'm here for," the brunette says.

She couldn't be more than seventeen.

"Great, what would you recommend?" I ask.

She doesn't miss a beat, "Hot or cold?"

I notice her nametag reads Molly. She smiles while she waits for me to answer, busying herself by wiping the counter at the same time.

"Hot," I respond.

I didn't realize it was possible, but her grin got even bigger like that's what she hoped I would say.

"Oh, then I would definitely recommend our chai latte. The chai we use is local and some of the best I've ever tasted, just the right amount of sweetness and spice." She tells me enthusiastically as she grabs a cup.

"I'll take it," I tell her. How could I resist her enthusiasm for a hot beverage?

"You got it," she says as she makes my drink.

I look around the small shop as she works. Different coffee-related items are hanging from the walls. Framed coffee pun quotes and pictures of different people enjoying a beverage right here in this shop. It's the perfect local coffee shop setting.

My thoughts are interrupted when the young barista asks me a question. "So, where are you visiting from?"

I turn my gaze toward her as she steams the milk. "I actually just moved here from Texas," I tell her.

"Oh, that's exciting! I've always wanted to go to Texas…you know, cowboys and all," she says as she waggles her eyebrows.

I can't help myself, and I burst out laughing. She looks at me with a grin spread wide across her face, apparently not offended at all that I'm laughing at her.

"Don't tell me Texas doesn't really have cowboys," she says.

Laughing, I say between giggles, "No…no, there are cowboys in some areas, but it is such a stereotype, and you said it in a way that gives me the idea you're romanticizing it."

"Well, yeah, aren't cowboys romantic?" she asks. She slides her drink across the counter to me. "That will be two fifty."

Reaching into my shoulder bag, I pull out a five-dollar bill. "Not at all," I tell her, still smiling. "Okay, maybe some of them, but they aren't any different than any other guy out there. They must be raised with some manners."

"I like your accent," she tells me matter-of-factly.

"Thank you. I like yours, too," I respond. I hand her the five-dollar bill. "Keep the change."

After she accepts the money, she reaches her hand across the counter. "I'm Molly. My parents own this shop."

I accept her hand and shake it, noticing it's slightly sticky. "I'm Maddie. It's nice to meet ya, Molly."

"Maddie...I like it," she says. "Maddie and Molly. I think we're meant to be friends."

Smiling, I say, "Well, Molly, I could use a friend. How old are you?"

"Fourteen," Molly tells me. "How old are you?"

"Twenty-six," I reply. "I loved being fourteen."

Molly gives me a look of disgust. I laugh. She rolls her eyes. I like this girl. I've laughed and smiled more in our fifteen-minute interaction than I have in a long time. I think I'm going to enjoy being friends with this fourteen-year-old girl.

The bell over the door rings, signaling another customer is walking through the door.

"Well, Molly, it was nice meeting you. I'm working

and living over at the Moonstone Bed and Breakfast. Be sure to stop by," I tell her as I make my way to the door to leave.

"Nice to meet you, Maddie. I'll be seeing you," Molly says.

I heard her greet the customer who had just walked in as I exited the shop. Taking my first sip of my chai, I sigh in contentment. Molly was right; just the right amount of sweetness and spice.

As if I suddenly remembered why I darted into the coffee shop, I glanced over my shoulder in the direction of where I last saw Ryder standing. But neither one of them is there.

Turning back toward the bed and breakfast, I leave thoughts of Ryder Evans behind me. Instead, I think of my new little town and my new friend, both filled with the kind of light I need in my life. Moving to Cambria feels right. I hope it's what I need to mend my broken pieces and find myself.

Ryder

Maddie Jennings has a boldness about her. I could see it in her the moment she came tearing around that porch this morning, and in the way, she pushed her shoulders back once she saw me outside my shop with Becca Taylor. I'm generally good at reading people, but this girl has a mystery about her. Maddie appears strong, yet there's a vulnerability to her. I can't quite pinpoint who she is and why she's here. She seems to hold back that part of her, though.

It's almost as if she's trying to hide it, too.

I watched as she glanced in my direction again when she left the shop. She couldn't see me, but I could see her.

"Yo, Ryder!" Billy says above me as I lie under the front of the car I'm working on, pulling me from my thoughts.

"Yeah, what is it?" I answer.

"Mrs. Beardsley is on the phone and wants to know if she can pick up her vehicle Monday morning instead of this afternoon," he asks.

"Sure, no problem. We need to make sure we lock it up in the garage," I tell him.

Billy is a good kid at nineteen. A lot like me when I was his age, unsure of where he wants to go in life, but knows he loves working on cars. He's good at it, too. I was happy when Sam decided to give him a chance. I can hear him telling Mrs. Beardsley we'll take care of her Suburban for her before hanging up.

I finish what I'm doing and slide out from under the car.

"Hey, Billy, hop in and give the key a turn," I tell him. He slides into the driver's side and turns the key, and the engine roars to life. "Let it run just a minute," I add. We listen to the engine running, and just as I hoped, the stutter is gone. "Okay, turn her off."

Billy does as I ask while I shut the hood. It's been a busy day today, and ending the workday on a good note feels good. I still have another car to work on today and am anxious to get there.

"You think you can lock up by yourself tonight?" I ask.

He grins at me, "Serious?" he questions. Only Sam and I have locked up the garage. It's a rule of thumb for us, but Billy has been here for six months. He's proven himself to be trustworthy and detail-oriented. I think he can handle it, and there's only one way to find out.

"Yep, I'm serious. I need to get over to my grandparents to change a fuse on their new employee's car. I want to get to it before the sun goes down," I tell him.

"I can do it," he states.

"I know. That's why I asked," I say, smiling back at him.

I grab a towel and wipe my hands. Then I turn to Billy and reach my fist out for a bump. He reciprocates the gesture. "The keys are on the hook; bring them Monday morning. See you then," I say, walking away.

"Got it. See you Monday," he tells me.

I walk out the door on the backside of the garage. The sun is just beginning its descent, and the usual ocean breeze is starting to cool the air.

Hopping in my truck, I pull away, thinking about the night ahead and the strange butterfly feeling I have in the pit of my stomach.

CHAPTER 5

Maddie

A bird flies low from tree to tree, singing a sweet little melody as I tip the rocking chair back and forth slowly. A smile creeps across my face. It's been a good day. It is the kind of day I've been longing to experience for some time. Peaceful is the only way to describe the sensation I'm feeling. When I left Texas, I wasn't sure what I was looking to find. Maybe it is as simple as this feeling I'm having now. Perhaps it will take a little longer for me to find it.

The crunch of gravel beneath tires pulls me from my thoughts.

Turning toward the sound behind me, I see Ryder climbing out of his pickup truck. His long, lean body is something to admire. Our eyes meet, so I raise my hand in a small gesture of greeting. He does the same with a crooked smile to go along with it. Neither of us exchanged words; instead, he went directly to my car, I assume, to do whatever he deemed necessary to fix it this morning.

So, instead of bothering him, I turn my mind back to my thoughts and the open, green backyard.

Growing up in a small Texas town, I'm used to open spaces: trees and the rolling hills of central Texas. My family's backyard is a large pasture. There is space here at Evelyn and Henry's, but it isn't as wide. But it's perfect.

I continue tipping the rocking chair with my foot as I allow my eyes to close. Taking a deep breath and releasing it in a long, drawn-out sigh, I let my mind clear, and my body relaxes—a feeling of happiness curls around my heart.

• • •

My eyes suddenly flash open when a gentle touch glides across my hair. I must have drifted to sleep because I feel a bit disoriented.

Ryder.

I'm shocked to find him standing over me, his hand resting softly on my head and his eyes wide. If I'm reading the look on his face right, he's a bit startled himself. He moves his hand quickly and stuffs it into his jeans pocket.

Stuttering, he says, "Sor...ry, you...I...you just looked so peaceful, and I don't know...I'm sorry."

Straightening myself up, I felt the need to reach up and touch the spot where his hand rested. Then suddenly, I remembered he was still standing there watching me. "Oh, uh..." I'm unsure what to say, but I know I don't want him to feel sorry. But words are stuck in my throat, so I only stare back at him dumbly.

"I'll see you up at the house," he says, finally breaking the awkward silence I have left between us. Ryder quickly turns on his heels toward his grandparents' house. I don't want him to go with this weirdness between us.

"Ryder!" I shout a little too loudly, standing up in the process. He stops in his tracks and pivots back in my direction, watching me with a look of curiosity, but he doesn't say anything, and I don't give him time to say anything. "Ryder," I say again, quieter this time. "Thank you."

His eyebrow raises in question. "For what?"

"For fixing my car," I answer. "I mean, I assume it's fixed."

Ryder allows a small smile to stretch his lips. "You're welcome." Then he turns back to head toward the front house. Without turning around, he calls over his shoulder, "I imagine dinner will be ready shortly. You might want to head this way soon yourself." He doesn't turn back around the entire way across the lawn, not even when he reaches the door. He simply walks through without a second glance. And I stand in the same place on my porch, unable to look away.

I know he's right about dinner when I glance at my watch. Five thirty. Evelyn told me this morning dinner would be between five thirty and six. But I need a moment to collect myself. I'm feeling a little off after that encounter. It seems like nothing, and everything happened in the span of a single minute. Ryder appeared to be as surprised by the moment as I was, but that didn't last long. What is it supposed to mean anyway? We just met this morning, yet it all seemed a bit too intimate.

Rolling my eyes at myself, I turn for the door to clean myself up quickly. I can't understand why I always overthink everything. Here I am, thinking about a man I barely know and trying to decipher a simple touch on my head as if he pulled me into his arms and kissed me.

Never mind the shiver that just ran up my spine at the thought.

Ryder

I take a deep breath as I close the door behind me. I tried massaging away the tension in my neck that rushed up my spine when Maddie's eyes flashed open. I don't know what I thought when I reached down to touch her. She just looked so damn beautiful. Peaceful. It was like I couldn't help myself. I needed to know if her auburn hair was as soft as it looked, the fiery strands glistening in the light from the setting sun. It almost felt like I had no choice, so I took liberty and got caught without thinking.

Now I'm kicking myself because I was so startled that I couldn't explain myself. I think I may have scared her. I'm such an asshole.

"Ry, is there a reason you're standing in the hall muttering to yourself?" My grandfather's voice startles me from my self-loathing spiral. "Your grandmother is just about ready for some help setting the table. Did you see Maddie out there?" He fires off questions in his typical fashion.

"Uh, just thinking," I answer the first of his questions, moving with him toward the kitchen. "And yes, sir, I did. I think she will be heading this way soon."

"Hope you're not thinking too hard," he quips as we enter the kitchen.

My grandmother moves around the kitchen effortlessly as she puts all the final touches on dinner. Without looking up from what she's doing, Grandma asks, "You've got something on your mind, Ryder?" She hands my grandfather a stack of plates with utensils and napkins on top.

Good lord, these two don't miss anything. You would think I would get used to it after all these years.

"Nothing too serious, Gran," I tell her, taking the four glass tumblers she set on the counter to bring to the table. Once I have all four in hand, I place one in each setting Grandad has laid out.

"Knock…knock," Maddie's voice echoes from the hallway leading from the back door. The tension I felt earlier zips up my spine again. She appears from around the corner in the kitchen doorway. "Good evening. I hope I'm not late."

Gran wipes her hands on her apron and walks over to Maddie to greet her properly. "Not at all, sweetie." Gran takes both of Maddie's hands into hers and pats them lightly. "How was your walk to Main Street?"

Grandad chimes in before she can answer Gran, "Did you make it into the coffee house?"

"Man, you two are like the Spanish Inquisition. Let her get both feet in the kitchen before you start in," I laugh.

Grandad and Maddie laugh while Gran rolls her eyes

and shushes me.

I had avoided meeting her eyes until now. Maddie is smiling and laughing, but when her gaze meets mine, she stops and clears her throat, quickly turning her attention away from me. "Well, I don't mind the inquisition so much. I have to say, the main street is adorable. I love the shops, and yes, I went to the coffee shop. I met the owner's daughter, Molly. She was so sweet," Maddie tells us. She keeps her eyes on my grandparents and off me.

"Aha, little Molly Miller. Sweet as she is chatty," Grandad says, a grin spread across his face.

"She has been a charmer since she could talk," Gran adds. "Her parents are good people." The timer on the oven suddenly goes off, causing Gran to jump and clasp her hands together. "Dinner bell just rang. Ryder, please bring the pitcher of water to the table."

Doing as I'm told, I grab the pitcher from the countertop where Gran had placed it. Taking it over to the table, I pour water into each glass I set at each place setting moments ago.

From behind me, I hear Maddie ask, "Can I do anything to help?"

"I believe everything has been handled," Gran tells her as she removes the roasted chicken from the oven, the smell permeating the room.

From the corner of my eye, I glimpse Maddie. She is watching my grandmother move around the kitchen. "Oh, well, if you're sure," Maddie says.

"Shall we sit, everyone?" Grandad asks. "Sit anywhere you would like, Maddie."

We all take our seats at the table; Grandad says grace, and then we all begin to serve ourselves. I like how comfortable Maddie seems at the table, like she has been here for years.

"This all looks and smells so good," Maddie says aloud. Her words and the smile displayed across her face are filled with sincerity. "I don't even know what to try first," she remarks, and I can't help the smile that crosses my face. Maddie's Southern draw and charm affect me. I can't seem to take my eyes off her.

"Take as much as you want," Gran tells her.

"Oh, I will. I'm unsure if I will listen to my eyes or my stomach. My eyes tend to win out in these situations."

Grandpa titters, "I know the feeling if my pants give any indication of just how often."

As soon as we have our plates loaded up, a brief silence settles among us as we savor our first taste of the meal.

"This is delicious. Thank you for having me over," Maddie compliments her, and Gran beams at Maddie between bites.

"I don't think Gran has ever cooked a bad meal in her life," I say.

"Well, there was that one time," Grandad says. Gran and I stop mid-bite and look to the end of the table where he sits. Maddie glances in his direction, too, and when they make eye contact, he gives her a wink.

She bursts out laughing. A full belly laugh, snort and all.

It's the best sound I've heard in a long time and apparently contagious because the rest of us laugh in no time.

"Henry, it seems you're looking to cook your own dinners for the rest of your life." This time, it's Gran's turn to give Maddie a wink.

Grandad's fork drops on his plate, "Now, Evelyn. You know I'm just kidding."

"Do I?" she says teasingly.

"You do. And don't act like you don't. Why do you have to go and ruin all the fun by saying something crazy like that?"

The conversation bounces between each end of the table. Maddie looks down at her food, holding back a grin. Once again, I find myself unable to take my eyes off her.

"If you can be funny, then so can I. Not to mention, I need to eat too, and I surely don't want you to cook my dinner." Gran smiles. "Maddie, Henry can do almost anything, but cooking is not his forte."

Grandad picks up his fork. Releasing a huff, he grunts, "That wasn't funny."

"Grandad, I hate to break it to you, but you had it coming. After all these years, I'm unsure why you haven't realized Gran always has the last laugh." I grin. My grandmother reaches over and pats my hand. Grandad rolls his eyes. When I glance in Maddie's direction, she looks at me with a bright smile. And for some reason, that simple look warms me to my very core.

There is something about this woman that is stirring up feelings deep inside of me. I wonder if I'm ready for it.

CHAPTER 6

Maddie

When I walk up to the house at eight o'clock, I'm excited for the day and fueled by a hot cup of coffee and pure adrenaline. Thank goodness because Evelyn and Henry weren't kidding when they said today would be jam-packed with check-ins.

The guest won't arrive for a few hours, so Evelyn reviews how things work. We look over the calendar and the check-in software. We check email and even review reservations to prepare ourselves for who will stay with us today.

The bed and breakfast goes from empty to full in no time. I barely have time to think, let alone sit and grab a bite to eat once check-in begins at eleven.

People are here traveling from all over. Some are from other parts of California, both north and south. A couple from New Hampshire on an anniversary getaway. Another from Arizona. And even one from British Columbia, Canada. All are kind and grateful for the quaint, cozy atmosphere we will provide during their stay.

I show them around and ensure they have everything they need. I provide them with the daily agenda of mealtimes, which are optional but part of their package.

Once I finally have everyone settled in, it's one o'clock, and I'm starving. My stomach grumbles, letting me know I wasn't happy I had neglected it. Note to self: I need to remember to plan better so I have something more than a cup of coffee for breakfast. Another roar comes from my middle section, and I swear it's my mama reminding me that breakfast is the most important meal of the day.

I know, Mama, I say aloud as I walk through the kitchen doorway.

"Was the day so crazy you're talking to yourself now?"

Startled, I jump, placing my hand over my heart. "God!"

"Nope, just me. Not to mention, from what I know, God is a man." When I look over at the kitchen table, I find a petite brunette sitting at the table nibbling on a cookie, looking up from her phone. She stands, wiping her hand on her pants before reaching out to me in greeting. "Sorry about that; I didn't mean to scare you. I'm Ros."

"Uh…hi, I'm…"

"Maddie. Yeah, I know. Grandad and Gran told me all about you. I saw you at the front desk when I came in this morning." She sits back down.

"Nice to meet you, Ros." I grab a water bottle from the pantry and then move toward the table. "Do you mind?" I ask, pointing at the chair opposite her at the kitchen table.

"Nope." She slides the plate of cookies across the table to me, leaning back in her chair and propping her feet up on the table.

"Thanks." I take a cookie from the plate and break a piece off.

"Looks like you could use some sustenance. You'll get used to it; I promise."

"Yeah, I'm not sure what I expected. I'm exhausted, but I loved it." I tell her. She smiles and keeps scrolling on her phone. "So...you're another grandkid, huh?"

"Yep, I guess you met my brother?"

"If Ryder is your brother, then yes, I did." I grab another cookie from the plate.

"That's the one," she answers.

"Are you just visiting?"

"I live up the street with a couple of roommates. I swing by to help in the kitchen a few days a week when I'm not in class for grad school."

"That's sweet of you."

She looks up and shrugs. "I try. They're pretty amazing grandparents, and they've always been here for me and Ry. I like my space, though, so I moved out."

Ros comes across as open and straightforward. I could already tell I liked her, and I only just met her. She seems close to my age, maybe a year or so younger.

"Rosalind May Evans, get your feet off my table!" Evelyn's voice echoes from behind me. Ros quickly removes her feet and sits up straight in her chair. "Sorry, Gran." Rosalind and I make eye contact and see a smiling gleam in her eye.

"Well, Maddie, how do you feel it went today? Think you made the right choice taking this job?" Evelyn walks around the table, grabbing a cookie from the plate as she sits beside Ros.

"Best first day I've had in years. I loved every busy, chaotic moment," I tell her. She gives me a warm smile, letting me know I just made her happy. "I think I will be able to make myself useful as I get the hang of things."

Clasping her hands together, Evelyn stands up. "I've got some things to finish up in my office. Rosalind, break is over. Back to work." She winks at me as she pats her granddaughter on the shoulder affectionately.

Ros rolls her eyes and stands up, then allows a slight grin to cross her face. "Can never get away with a thing around that one." As she follows in the direction Evelyn disappeared, Ros says over her shoulder, "Nice to meet you, Maddie."

"Nice to meet you, too," I call after her.

Glancing at my watch, I sigh when I see it is fifteen till two. Breaks over for me soon, too. I grab one last cookie and my water, then return to my desk to finalize next month's reservations and answer emails before I get off in a few hours.

● ● ●

I walk the block into town to grab a few things from the store when I get off work. I can't expect Evelyn to cook for me every night, although she invited me when I went to her office to let her know I was leaving for the day.

As I walked back to my cottage, I noticed a slight breeze moving in, so I put on a light sweater. Something I would never need to do in the middle of June in Texas. This makes me smile, which is strange because I miss home so much. I think I'm smiling because, while I long for my family and the familiarity of my old life, I like this place. The weather. The people I've met.

Just as that thought crosses my mind, I hear someone calling my name from behind, so I turn around. About twenty feet in the distance, Molly Miller, the barista, is waving at me. "Maddie!"

Waving back, I wait for her to catch up. "Hey, Molly, heading to town?" I ask her once she's closer.

"Yep, I have to close the coffee shop tonight."

"What time do you close?"

"We're open until seven-thirty. I help my mom out so she can go to the back and work on bookkeeping stuff while I handle the front."

"Aha, I see. It's pretty sweet of you to help out like you do."

Molly shrugs her shoulders. "I don't mind really. What else is there for a fourteen-year-old to do in this town?"

"I can see your point. Well, I think I might need to drop in. I haven't stopped thinking about that white mocha chai you made me," I tell her.

"Told ya it's good."

"You did. It was more than good. It was sinful!" We continued to walk side by side down the tree-lined sidewalk until we reached the main street. "Well, I'm going to head into the market, but I will come by to see you before

I head back home."

"Cool," Molly says, walking backward to face me while moving toward her family's coffee shop. "See you soon."

"See ya." We parted ways, and as I walked the rest of the way to the market, I noticed the town's quiet on a Monday evening compared to the weekend. Tourists are sparse since most shops close reasonably early around here, and the streets seem filled with locals.

I pull out the shortlist I made before leaving the house as I enter the store's produce section, glancing over each item to ensure I don't forget anything. Suddenly, I feel someone to my left, and when I look up, I take a startled step back.

"Sorry, I didn't mean to scare you."

Ryder.

I recover quickly, laughing. "You didn't scare me; I wasn't expecting you."

"Yeah, you were studying that paper pretty intensely."

Holding it in the air between us, I say, "Oh, my grocery list. I wanted to remind myself of what I had on it so I don't forget anything. I always seem to forget something, even with a list," I laugh again at myself. Ryder's grin gets wider. He is incredibly handsome.

"Yeah, well, I don't even make a list. I just come here hoping to get what I don't have at home and enough to make a complete meal." This time, we both laugh.

There is a split second where we both stare at one another in silence. The memory of our encounter last night creeps in, and I can't help the blush I feel moving into my cheeks. Before he noticed, I decided to excuse myself.

"Well, nice seeing you," I tell him and turn to walk away.

"Maddie."

I pivot to face him once again.

"Yeah?"

"Wanna grab something to eat from the deli at Dream Bean Cafe?"

Oh God, does he mean now? Or just another time? There it is again. That strange feeling, like he sees to the center of my heart. My body reacts to Ryder Evans. A sort of tingling sensation moves through me, and I wonder if he can also see my body's reaction to him when he looks at me.

"Uh, ummm," I stammer. "Uh, sure, we can do that sometime."

"How about right now?"

I glance around us nervously, then back at Ryder. "Now?" Okay, Madelyn. He meant right now. I don't know why I'm feeling so nervous. I guess it's because he's a stranger, and I'm a blushing fool. Not to mention, there hasn't been a single guy to give me goosebumps and butterflies since I was nearly fourteen years old when Connor asked me to my first middle school dance.

"Yes," he states matter-of-factly. Then, he allows the silence to hang between us.

At first, I don't respond. I stare back into his eyes. I don't know what I'm trying to see, but I want to catch a glimpse of what I think he sees in me. Is Ryder asking me on a date? Am I ready for a date? I'm getting ahead of myself. He's being friendly because he knows I don't know anyone here. I observe his calm composure. His handsome face is waiting for an answer to a simple question. Good lord, Madelyn, quit worrying about things that may not even matter.

"Look, Maddie, it's just dinner. I want to get to know you better, that's all. You're new in town, and I could always use a new friend. It's the gentlemanly thing to do. I'll even walk you back to the store so we can finish our grocery shopping after. It is just a half a block down from here."

Tucking a strand of loose hair behind my ear, I continue scanning his gaze and only see the sincerity in him. "Okay," I finally respond. "That would be nice." A smile quickly appears on his face, and I allow myself to return the gesture. I've had difficulty letting down my guard since Connor's betrayal nine months ago. But Ryder is right. I could use a friend. Friends are safe.

CHAPTER 7

Ryder

I'm sure Maddie is confused by my invitation. Honestly, I'm surprised, too. We met two days ago, so this seems out of left field. Luckily, the "you need a friend" comment works to help make sense of it. Or at least that's what I'm going to tell myself. And as long as she doesn't call me out, it will remain my truth.

The real truth is I have no idea why I proposed dinner in the middle of the grocery store.

I can tell she is waiting for me to move. So, I say, "Good, because I didn't feel like cooking either, so you're saving me. If that tells you anything, I cook more like Grandad than Gran." I wink as I wave my hand for her to move toward the grocery store exit.

When we reach the doors, we put our little baskets away and continue into the cool evening.

At first, Maddie and I walked down the sidewalk toward Dream Bean Cafe in comfortable silence.

"So, Gran and Grandad didn't say what brought you all the way to California for a job at some little family-owned bed and breakfast," I ask, breaking the silence. It's something I've been wondering about, and it felt like an easy start to get to know her. If I don't know anything else, the one thing I do know is I would like to get to know Maddie.

I hear a quiet sigh before she takes a deep breath and answers, "Well, I needed a change. A change of pace. Of scenery."

She sighed again, and I could tell she wasn't finished. "You see when you grow up in a tiny town with one stop light, where everyone knows your name, your parents, your siblings, even your birthday, it's easy to lose yourself in that completely. Especially when you have your whole life planned out from a young age, and then your naïve dream is crushed." She lets out a small laugh.

"Whoa, I guess that was a loaded question."

She looks over at me and stops walking. I stop, too, and watch her.

"Sorry about that," she continued. "I guess I could've simply said I want to find out who I am without everyone else telling me who that is."

"Maddie, never apologize to me for being honest," I tell her. She gives me a slight nod of her head and a smile. "Shall we?" I ask, motioning down the sidewalk in the direction we were moving.

I begin walking but suddenly realize Maddie isn't with me. When I turned back, she stared at me with a look I couldn't decipher. Her eyes tell me she's far away in her thoughts, but she focuses on me. Instead of saying anything, I allow her to have this moment, and while her gaze is on me, I'm strangely comfortable in her scrutiny. Our eyes lock, both trying to see what is beyond the surface. Whatever I did or said moments ago opened a door I didn't know was closed. Let alone exist. "Maddie?" I finally interrupt the unspoken conversation between us.

She blinks, and she's back here on the sidewalk with me. Her hand nervously brushes the hair that had fallen across her forehead.

"Sorry, I don't know where my mind just went," she says. I don't believe her. She knows; she just isn't ready to take me there with her. She puts a smile on her face, walking to catch up with me. When she's even with me again, I fall into step with her. I can see by the look on her face she's thankful I didn't ask questions about what just happened.

A minute later, I'm pulling open the door to Dream Bean Cafe. Maddie gives me a nod of thanks as I step to the side for her to enter first.

"Mmmm, I love the smell of coffee and baked goods," she says when I step in behind her.

"I can't say I disagree," I laugh.

An empty table in the back catches my notice, and just before I say anything to Maddie, a wide-eyed teenager is standing before us. "Maddie! Ryder!" Molly beams.

"I was hoping my favorite Molly Miller would be working tonight," I say in greeting. Her grin grows wider, and her cheeks turn a light shade of pink.

"Hey, Molly," Maddie says. Molly's gaze zips from me to Maddie. "What can I get you two?" Molly asks as she makes her way behind the counter to serve us.

"What is the soup of the day?" I ask.

"Tomato bisque," Molly answers.

It's one of my favorites. I look over to Maddie, "It's delicious and the best in town, in my opinion. I think I'm going to get a bowl with grilled cheese on sourdough. What are you in the mood for?"

"Actually, that sounds pretty amazing. I don't think I've had that since I was a kid," she tells me.

Looking over at Molly, I ask, "You got that?"

"I'm on it," she replies. "I'll bring it over when I have it ready. You can pay me later."

"Perfect, thanks, Molly." When I look back at Maddie, she glances around the room. "I saw a booth in the back when we first walked in, and it's still open. Is that okay with you?" I point toward the table, and Maddie's gaze follows.

"Yeah, of course," she tells me.

Maddie led the way, and as we made our way to the table, I noticed several tables of locals watching us with interest. "Good evening, Mrs. Rogers," I say to our infamous town gossip. "Nice to see you as always."

"Nice to see you," she pauses before glancing briefly at Maddie, "and your new friend, Ryder." Reluctantly, I realize the only way to beat gossip is to face them head-on. Otherwise, they get to make up the words that fill your story. I stopped next to her table and took hold of Maddie's hand to stop her, too, and she turned her back to me. "Mrs. Rogers, this is Maddie Jennings. She just moved to town and works for my Gran and Grandad at the bed and

47

breakfast."

"Welcome to Cambria. It's always nice to have a newbie in our quaint little town," Mrs. Rogers says sweetly while eyeing Maddie up and down.

Maddie places a bright and sincere smile on her face as she sticks her hand out in greeting. "Nice to meet you. And thank you, I love it so far."

"Well, isn't that accent just the cutest," Mrs. Rogers says.

Maddie blushes and pushes a strand of her long, auburn hair behind her ear.

"Yes, it is," I respond, keeping my eyes on Maddie. "Well, we're going to get our seats."

Maddie gave the older woman a small wave, and we continued to our table.

I allow Maddie to sit first, then take the seat opposite her. "She seems nice," Maddie says.

Chuckling, I say, "Yeah, something like that. Remember, small, town gossip doesn't only happen in the South."

"Her being nice has nothing to do with being a gossip," Maddie grins, giving me a wink. "I can handle a town gossip any day. It's the mean ones who I can't keep up with."

I laugh out loud this time.

"Tell me more about you. Right now, I only know you are sweet to my grandparents and that you have a beautiful smile and a fiery temper when woken up," I tease.

"Hey! In my defense, I woke up in a strange place and didn't know who you were," she exclaims.

"Okay...okay, I will hold my judgment on your morning temper until I know you a little better." I stare at her expectantly.

She shifts nervously under my gaze. "What? Why are you looking at me that way?"

"I'm waiting for you to start revealing just who Maddie Jennings is," I clarify.

She giggles, and the sound reaches into my chest like it's trying to hug my heart. The sound is soothing and makes me feel the carefree joy behind it. I promised myself right then to make sure I always do what it takes to make her laugh as much as possible.

"Fine, what do you want to know, Mr. Evans?" she retorts.

I tap my index finger to my chin and look at the ceiling like I'm thinking hard about the perfect question. After a few seconds, I look directly into her eyes, "What's your favorite color?" I ask, my tone serious.

She bursts out laughing. "Seriously? That's the first thing you want to know about me?"

"Well, I already know the important starter things, like your name, where you're from, your job," I pause before continuing. "What you look like the moment you get out of bed." A slow grin creeps across my face.

Maddie laughs out loud again. "Boy, you're not gonna let me live that down, are you?"

My smile widens. "Nope, probably not."

"Fine," she says. "Yellow. But not just any yellow. A light buttery yellow."

"Huh…yeah, that's a nice color. Happy," I tell her. "Who…"

"Oh, no, you don't!" she interrupts. "It's my turn."

"Your turn?" I question.

She wags her finger at me. "You're not the only one who gets to ask the questions."

I throw my hands up in front of me in a faux defensive gesture. "Okay...okay, we'll take turns."

She places her hands on the table before her, lacing her fingers together. Her features set in what I imagine a police interrogator would look like while interviewing a suspect.

"How old were you when you had your first..." She pauses, and my eyebrows raise. "Airplane ride." It's my turn to laugh this time.

Shaking my head, I say, "When I was seven, we flew to Hawaii for a family vacation with Gran and Grandad."

Maddie gets a dreamy look in her eyes. "I've always wanted to go to Hawaii."

"It's a beautiful place," I share. Her lips tip up at the corners.

I immediately go into my next question, "What's your favorite place you've ever been?"

"That's easy to answer, Key West," she responds.

"Nice, I've never been, but I've always wanted to go," I divulge.

We continued our banter of questions with simple and everyday inquiries as we started. We laugh at ones that reveal childhood crushes and adolescent dreams of when we grew up. In between, Molly brought us our food and, surprisingly, never interrupted our conversation.

Before we knew it, two hours passed, and our food had long disappeared. We only realized the time when, from the corner of my eye, I spotted Molly turning the chairs upside down on the tables.

"Looks like we have almost overstayed our welcome," I joke.

Maddie looks in the direction I'm staring. We both glance at our watches.

"Wow," she grins. "This has been fun. Thank you. I think this was just what I needed."

"Me, too," I tell her.

We both stand, carrying our plates to the dirty dish bin next to the counter.

"Molly, thanks for the dinner and pleasant atmosphere," I yell over my shoulder at the teen.

"Yep, not sure I had anything to do with the pleasant atmosphere," she tells me. When I look at her, Molly is again bouncing between me and Maddie.

"Yeah, maybe you're right," I react.

Maddie looks over at me. Our eyes lock, and we both regard one another for a beat.

Looking away, Maddie says abruptly, "I better get home." I don't say anything in return. I follow her to the door.

We bid Molly farewell as we exited the café, and she locked it behind us.

The sun had already set, and the streetlamps that lined the main street were illuminating our tiny little town.

Maddie faces me, fidgeting with her hair in a way I've seen her do many times over the two days I've known her. "Well, thanks again for tonight. It was fun," she says.

"It was," I reply. "And I'm walking you to the store, remember?"

"It's okay; I've decided to go tomorrow or another day this week."

"Then, I'm walking you home. There is no way I'm letting you walk alone."

"Oh, gosh, Ryder," she says as she steps back. "You don't need to do that. Isn't your apartment just there above your shop?"

"It is, and I do need to," I insist. "My Gran and Grandad taught me manners."

Maddie rolls her eyes, "Fine." She turned toward the bed and breakfast, and I followed.

Soon, we match our strides and walk side by side in a comfortable silence.

I wonder what she is thinking. My mind is full of more questions, but I keep those stored away for a different time.

We don't say anything for the entire five-minute walk to her cottage. I stay with Maddie on her front porch.

When we got to the door, Maddie reached for the doorknob, pausing to look back at me—silence between us. My heart starts to beat at a different rhythm than it has before.

"Well, thanks again," she says nervously.

"Maddie, you don't have to keep thanking me," I tell her.

"Sorry," she says.

"Don't keep apologizing either," I grin. Her lips turn up at the corners, too.

She begins to say something again, then snaps her lips together. I have a feeling she was about to apologize again.

"Good night, Maddie. It was a nice night," I finally say, leaning forward. Her eyes go wide, then close. My heartbeat speeds up a little more because I think she's permitting me to kiss her. Not yet, I tell myself. This time needs to be different. She's different. So, instead of placing my lips against hers, I lightly brush them to the side of her cheek. I hear a soft sigh escape between her lips as I pull away. When I open my eyes, hers are still closed.

Her eyes flash open as she takes a step back. I don't say a word, and I don't turn around. I keep taking small steps backward, watching her until I reach the edge of the porch.

"Good night, Ryder," she finally says in a whisper just before I turn and leave.

CHAPTER 8

Maddie

My mind is on one thing as I walk through the bed and breakfast kitchen door. Caffeine. I need caffeine like I need air to breathe this morning. I pushed the brew button on the coffeemaker that was waiting for someone to start it. Pulling the cabinet door open, I grab a mug and set it on the counter. Now I wait.

Leaning over the counter, I place my chin into my hands, closing my eyes. I sigh. After Ryder left last night, I couldn't sleep. My mind raced around like an Indy car on a racetrack.

Instead of sleeping, I lay in bed, eyes wide, unable to relax enough to fall asleep.

"Morning," I hear from behind me.

When I turned around, I found Ros Evans walking across the kitchen. She looks fresh and full of smiles.

"Morning," I say with as much perk I can muster.

"Not much sleep, huh?" Ros asks.

I yawn as if on cue, giving myself away. "Nope," I answer in confirmation.

She takes a mug from the cabinet and turns toward me, leaning against the counter next to me. "Are you finding it hard to settle into a new place? I would have trouble doing it myself."

Shrugging, I tell her, "I'm not real sure. That must be it." I lied. Settling in here has been surprisingly easy. I didn't realize until I got to Cambria just how badly I needed to get away. I don't want to tell her that her brother is the reason for my lack of sleep. Feelings that only one other person has ever evoked in me suddenly coursed through my body when his lips touched my cheek last night. If I'm honest, it was probably the moment he asked me to dinner last night. But I can't tell Ros any of that, so this little white lie will have to do, and she seems to accept it.

The coffee is finally done. Ros grabs the pot and kindly offers to pour me the first cup.

"Thanks," I say, closing my eyes as I take a deep inhale through my nose. I love the smell of freshly brewed coffee in the morning.

She pours herself a cup and smiles, "You look like you need it more than me. Not to mention, you hit the brew button first."

Blowing on the hot liquid before taking my first sip, I sigh deeply. "Coffee is life," I say aloud.

Ros takes a sip herself and nods in agreement. "You can say that again."

As Evelyn glides into the room, we're both suddenly pulled from our euphoric thoughts.

"Morning, ladies. I hope you saved a cup for me."

Before she reaches us, I pull a cup from the cupboard, and Ros pours the coffee. I turn to hand it to Evelyn when she's close enough. "If you would've been even a minute later, you may have missed out," I tease. Evelyn grinned, and we all sat at the table to review our day.

I miss my mama and daddy. I miss my family and friends. But it's easy being here at the bed and breakfast and in this town…with these people.

And isn't that part of my problem? It was just too easy to be with Ryder last night.

• • •

I push the door closed with my hip as I enter the cottage with my arms full of grocery bags.

After work, I made it to the store and checked off all the items on my list. Of course, Evelyn invited me to dinner tonight, but I told her I had some unpacking to finish so that I would make something quick for myself. She reluctantly accepted. And I allowed myself to believe my tiny lie was the real reason I skipped out on a home-cooked meal, and it had nothing to do with the possibility of running into Ryder.

Placing the bags on the kitchen island, I unload the groceries one thing at a time.

I came here to find myself and who I am through my eyes. Not to become the girl living life through another's vision. Yet, after only two days and one dinner, feelings I haven't truly felt in years are bubbling to the surface.

I need to be different, not someone who loses themselves in another person again. I could see losing myself in Ryder Evans: his charm, his honesty, and that crooked smile. I could easily and happily get lost in all of him until it wasn't easy or happy.

And that scares me.

I closed the fridge after I placed the juice on the top shelf. Picking up my phone, I scroll through my social media aimlessly when my phone rings and my sister's face pops up on the screen.

"How do you do it?" I ask when I tap the accept button and put the phone to my ear. As I settle in, I walk over the couch and curl my legs under me.

"Be amazing?" she asks without skipping a beat. "I guess I was just born that way."

I roll my eyes at her answer, even though she can't see me. Caroline is quick with her silly sarcasm. "You're amazing, but that isn't what I was referring to. I meant how you always know when I need you."

"You okay?" Caroline asks, her tone turning serious.

Caroline is six years older than me. We're as close as two sisters can be, and, in many ways, she's always been a little motherly to me.

"Yeah, I'm good. Just adjusting and determined to figure my crap out," I reassure her.

"Maddie, why do you act like you don't have your life together?" She sighs quietly through the phone before continuing, "You know who you are; you just put a lifetime of effort into someone who took you for granted."

"I don't want to talk about him," I say.

"Fine, then tell me what's bugging you," Caroline states, simply moving on. She has always been good at just letting me process things without pushing. I said I didn't want to talk about Connor, and she respected me enough not to push the subject.

"First, tell me what's happening at home," I tell her.

"Well, Jake is driving Mom and Dad crazy as usual. He can't seem to make up his mind about what he wants to do with his life. Mom and Dad are the same but miss you," she shares.

I laugh at the Jake comment because it doesn't surprise me. Our brother, Jake, three years younger than Caroline and three years older than me, has always moved to the beat of his drum. Never settling on anything in life. As for Mom and Dad missing me, I knew this already because they've texted me multiple times a day since I left, telling me so. It's just like Caroline to leave herself out when letting me in on life back home.

"And what about you?"

"Oh, Maddie, you know me. Just being a momaholic," she says casually.

Caroline is married to her college sweetheart and has two kids. My niece and nephew are probably the cutest people in my life. They adore me, and I love them. Honestly, leaving them was perhaps the most challenging part.

"Yes, I know you. And I would be a momaholic, too, if I had those two little monkeys for kids. Rob is pretty okay, too," I tell her. Rob, my brother-in-law, is nearly perfection. Kind, attentive, and completely head over heels in love with my sister. "But seriously, what's new in the

Adam's household."

"Really, there is nothing new, Maddie. It's the usual day-to-day. Eat, sleep, play dates, and if I'm lucky, late-night snuggles with Rob," She giggles, and I laugh with her. Our laughter is almost identical, so it sounds like an echo through the phone. "Tell me about Cambria, Mr. and Mrs. Evans, and the new job."

"Gosh, Caro. The town is just so adorable. It reminds me of one of those Hallmark romance movie towns." I know she will be able to picture it because we've spent many weekends binging those "cheesy love shows," as Jake always called them when he was teasing us. "Mr. and Mrs. Evans are as wonderful as I remember. Both sweet and funny and constantly trying to feed me. The job is exciting because it is new but seems right for me."

"It all sounds...perfect, Madds," she says, but I can hear some skepticism behind her words.

"It practically is, Caro. Everything and everyone is so welcoming and," I pause as my mind drifts to Ryder. "Welcoming and perfect," I finish.

"Everything and everyone, huh?" I can hear the suspicion in her voice.

"Yes, everything and everyone."

"What are you leaving out, Maddie?" Caroline asks. I could tell her nothing, and, like always, she wouldn't push. I could, but I won't because this is my sister. She is the one person I can say anything to, and she will listen and tell me what I need to hear. Not what I want to hear.

"The Evans's have a grandson, Ryder."

"A grandson...like a six-year-old?" she questions. "Or

a GRANDson," Caroline emphasizes the grand part of grandson. I imagine she is wiggling her eyebrows as she says this.

"The latter," I say, trying to sound nonchalant.

"Okay, this sounds interesting."

"Caro! I came here to figure out my crap. I didn't come here to get caught up in someone else."

"Maddie, you've been there for three days," she says, like she is stating something significant to what I'm feeling.

"I hear what you're saying, but Caro, you don't understand."

"Then help me," she replies.

"He gives me that butterfly feeling. He's honest and kind. He is helpful and...and...so freaking gorgeous."

"Oh, well, of course. The dreaded butterfly feeling." Her words are dripping with sarcasm.

"Caroline, I'm serious!"

"I can hear that, but why are you saying all those things like they're the most horrible qualities in a person?"

Her question is valid. She doesn't understand that it's not Ryder that is concerning me. It's how he makes me feel.

"You don't understand, it's Connor,"

"My God, Maddie, what the heck does Connor have to do with anything in Cambria? Leave him out of it. You left your home to be rid of that ass, don't bring him there with you," she scolds.

"I'm not...I didn't. It's not exactly Connor. I mean, I'm not pining for him or anything. When I say Connor, I mean

I'm scared I will never find what I'm looking for here. And I will lose myself in Ryder like I did with Connor." I spill every worry onto my sister.

"His name is Ryder?"

This is her response to everything I just said.

"Uh, yeah, but..."

"Even his name is sexy," she says.

"Good gracious, Caro," I say, then let a giggle escape. "I'm trying to be serious."

"So am I, Madds. It's been only a few days, and you're thinking about someone other than Connor. This is a win in my book. As for losing yourself, I don't think you were ever that lost. Who you are is pretty incredible."

"But..." I begin to say.

"No, listen to me. You don't need to be someone different. You only need to put yourself first for once. It would be best if you dreamed a little and took what you wanted. Maddie, it's time for you to see the world and how you fit in it through your eyes and not how others see it for you, especially Connor." Her words are firm but gentle and precisely what I need to hear.

There is silence between us. Another thing Caroline has always been good at is saying what needs to be told and then allowing you time to process it.

"Thanks, Caro. I love you."

"I love you, too, Maddie." She clears her throat. "Now, just take things day by day, and if that includes a certain sexy named man, then embrace it!"

I laugh because she isn't going to let that go.

"I gotta go, Madds. Rob and the kids just got home,

and chaos will soon ensue."

"Love you, Caroline, and thanks again for being such a good sister friend. Give Rob and my monkeys some love from me."

"Love you, too, Maddie. Be happy," she says before ending the call.

Be happy. It has been a while since I thought about being happy. Before, I just said I was happy, but was I? I never consciously thought about what makes me content in life. I was so busy trying to make Connor happy.

Since arriving in Cambria, I've felt happier than I can ever remember, as long as I don't overthink my feelings.

Maybe it is that simple. Be happy.

CHAPTER 9

Ryder

The glow of light from the cottage across the back lawn keeps my attention while I mindlessly dry the dish Ros just handed me. As I stare out the window, I can't help wondering what Maddie is doing.

If I'm honest, I only came over for dinner tonight, hoping to see her. When she wasn't here, and Gran said she wasn't coming, I was surprised by my intense disappointment.

I spent the entire day in the shop with my mind on our dinner last night. The feeling I had when I left her standing on the porch, her eyes asking me for something I'm not sure we are ready for. But I want just as much as she does.

There is no denying it—I want Maddie like I've never wanted another woman.

"Earth to Ryder!" Rosalind's voice breaks through my thoughts, and when I glance over, she is trying to hand me another dish. "I'm pretty sure that one is dry, and this one needs your drying skills. Where are you?"

My gaze drifts back out the kitchen window as I take the dish from her. "Sorry, I guess I spaced out."

"Dude, you're pining," Ros accuses.

My head snaps to Rosalind, whose mouth is gaping open. She's staring at me with her hands in a sudsy bowl. "I'm what?"

"You. Ryder. Michael. Evans. Are. Pining. Over. A. Girl." She annunciates each word that comes out of her mouth slowly as if I only read lips. A huge grin spreads across her face like she just won the lotto.

"I'm not pining," I deny.

"You are," she retorts.

"Am not."

"Are too."

"Am..." I start, but Grandad's voice stops me. "Did I go back in time, or are you two just channeling your five- and ten-year-old selves?"

"Nope, Ryder just..." I give Ros a look that stops her mid-sentence. "Ryder just thinks he can wash the dishes better and faster than I can." She grins at Grandad.

"Well, you're both wasting water and time," Grandad says.

"Sorry," we say in unison.

He picks up his reading glasses from the table, shaking his head as he glances back at us before walking out.

At first, neither of us say anything. We finish cleaning the dishes in silence.

Ros shuts off the water as I dry the last dish before putting it away. My attention drifts back across the backyard. From the corner of my eye, I can see Ros watching me. "You're pining, and I'm here for it," she says, walking away. Just before she is out of earshot, she calls over her shoulder, "Night, Ry."

Is Rosalind right? Am I pining? Maybe. Nah, I don't pine. But I do want Maddie Jennings. I want to know every part of her.

• • •

When I say my goodbyes to Gran and Grandad, I head out the front door and walk down the driveway toward home. I walked the quarter of a mile over after work rather than drive the short distance.

I'm near to the road when I come to a stop. Putting my hands on my hips, I allow my head to fall forward. There is a war going on in my mind about whether or not I will turn back around and head straight to the cottage to find out if Maddie has been thinking about me as much as I have her today.

I'm unsure how long I paced around the driveway before I finally decided to knock on her door and ask her out on an actual date. Not one where there's a pretense of something else.

As I reach the corner of the house, part of me hopes the light is off, and Maddie has gone to bed. The other part of me is worried the light won't be on, and she's gone to bed.

I keep my eyes on my feet as I round the corner until I finally make myself look up. The room is still glowing in the dark, indicating Maddie is still awake. Once again, I find myself frozen in place, contemplating.

"What the hell is wrong with you?" I mutter out loud to myself. "You've asked a woman out before." Picking my feet up, I move forward.

It's dark, and the air is cool, perfect. The sky is clear, allowing the stars to show off their shine. When I reach the front of the cottage, I walk up to the door, and the nerves hit me again.

I raise my hand to knock, then pull it back. "Shit," I whisper into the dark. "Don't be a coward, Ryder." I raise my hand to knock again, but before I can finish the motion, I'm startled by a voice to the right of me coming from the dark. "They say when you talk to yourself, you aren't crazy unless you answer."

"Shit!" I blurt out. "Maddie?"

A giggle carries through the darkness and wraps around me. "Sorry, I started saying something to you before you even exited the porch. I just didn't, and I thought you would see me."

"No…nope, didn't see you," I tell her as I approach her silhouette.

She stood up from the chair she was sitting in but didn't take a step toward me. I don't stop walking until I'm standing mere inches from her. Maddie sucks in a breath.

Maddie is nearly as tall as I am at six feet, so I only need to lower my gaze a couple of inches for our eyes to meet. And when they do, the look I see there pulls me in further. She bites her lower lips and quickly diverts her eyes away from mine, then back again. What in the hell is happening? "Ryder," she breathes. "I don't understand."

My eyes moved to her lips, where she was biting down and backing up again. "Neither do I," I confess. "Maddie, I think I need to kiss you." I am waiting for some sort of permission.

"Ryder, I think I need you to kiss me, too," she says huskily.

It's as if those words gave both of us the permission we were seeking because as I lower my mouth, she raises on her toes to meet me simultaneously. And when our lips touch, a surge of warmth and desire sweeps over me. We don't move to deepen the kiss; we hold still like we're savoring the sensation of our lips touching. As if on cue, as soon as that feeling envelopes me head to toe, I lightly press my tongue to her lips, and she opens willingly, allowing me to deepen the kiss. Maddie's hands move around my neck, and I pull her closer with mine. It's slow yet powerful, unlike any first kiss I've had before and not like the last one. As we pull away, I realize this is the only real kiss I've ever truly experienced.

When we've stopped and are again staring into one another's eyes, I say the first word that pops into my head. "Wow."

A grin spreads across her features, and my heart skips a beat. "I agree," she responds.

"I promise I came here to ask you out again. Officially."

"Okay," she says, a bit nervously.

I bring my hand up to cup her face. "There's something about you. I want to find out exactly what that is," I tell her. She leans her head into my palm and closes her eyes.

"Will you go to dinner with me, Maddie?" Her eyes open, but she doesn't say anything. I can see in her eyes that she is warring with something. "I know you just got here, and we've just met, but..."

"Yes," she interrupts me. "Yes, I will go to dinner with you."

Taking a quick step back, I run my hand through my hair, then I step back toward Maddie and pull her mouth to mine again. She comes willingly and responds like I'm giving her exactly what she wants.

Stepping back, I whisper, "I better go."

"You better go," she says like she's even less convinced of that decision than I am.

"I better go," I repeat, swiftly turning away and walking off the porch. She follows me to the edge, and I can finally see her. The moonlight glows just brightly enough for me to see her kiss-swollen lips. I notice she's in tiny shorts and a shirt with a cardigan. God, she is sexy.

"We'll talk tomorrow and work out dinner," I tell her.

She nods, "Tomorrow."

"I want to kiss you again," I say aloud. "But I won't because if I do, I won't be able to stop. So instead, I will say goodnight, walk home, and see you tomorrow." I take a step backward. She remains motionless.

"Goodnight, Maddie."

"Goodnight, Ryder, see you tomorrow."

I leave her standing there on that porch for the second night in a row. It seems like I've left a small part of me with her I didn't know existed each time.

CHAPTER 10

Maddie

Touching my fingertips to my lips, I watch Ryder walk away until he disappears from my line of sight. The last fifteen minutes were unexpected. Incredible but surprising.

When I got off the phone with Caroline earlier, I ate something, showered, and then decided to sit on the porch. I left the porch light off, so it was dark, which allowed me to see the stars even better. It's a beautiful night. Peaceful.

I thought about my conversation with Caroline and everything she said about my past and my new start here in Cambria. I was thinking about Ryder and how I was attracted to him from the moment I saw him. Then, every encounter I've had with him since the morning after I arrived, he's shown me more and more of the kind of guy he is. The more he shows me, the more I want to know.

The more attracted I am to him.

This is new to me. I've loved the same boy for nearly

my entire life. Connor. The only person I ever loved. I never even considered what being with someone else would be like. To care for anyone else. Until now. Until Ryder.

Not long ago, my life was so planned out. The hard part is I would've been happy with that plan. I would've loved Connor for the rest of my life. I would've married him, had his children, and cared for him forever without wishing for more.

But that's not what happened.

Instead, Connor changed our plans and broke his promises. He broke my heart and nearly broke me. He threw away everything we ever meant to one another for one moment...one night of pleasure. I never thought I would come back from that heartbreak, but my family carried me until I could stand on my own again.

One day, I woke up and decided I wouldn't live life for anyone other than myself again. Although I know this is best for me, a part of me will always love Connor and lose hope of what we could have had.

But it's the reason I came to Cambria. It's why I needed to find out who I am and what I want from life. I have too much pride in myself to do anything else.

Meeting a man or dating someone isn't part of figuring out who I am. I'm only just beginning this journey, and yet, Ryder has already caused a fork in the road of this new life I'm setting up for myself. But the way it feels to be kissed by him isn't something I can ignore.

I guess it doesn't matter what I have planned. Caroline says to trust myself and let go. Mama would say let go and let God. The theme seems to be to let go and trust.

If Ryder is standing at the end of this new road, I'm not confident I have a choice anyway.

I don't know how long I stood on the porch staring into the night, unable to move because everything that transpired moments ago felt like a dream.

It wasn't a dream, though. Ryder kissed me and changed everything.

Slowly, I make my way into the house, flipping the lights off behind me until I enter my room and crawl beneath the blanket.

Surprisingly, I'm feeling relaxed and something I haven't felt in a very long time—happy.

Smiling, I close my eyes and allow the exhaustion that has consumed me for nearly a year to pull me into the best sleep I've had in a very long time.

Ryder

It felt like I floated the entire walk home. Kissing Maddie was more than I ever envisioned it being. It felt natural and comforting but also hungry and full of desire. Her lips seemed to be made for mine.

I've kissed women, but this was beyond anything I've experienced.

I want more than just the physical satisfaction I'm sure we can give each other. Of course, I like that, too, but I need to know her beyond that.

When I reach my apartment above the shop, I unlock the door, throwing my keys on the table. Making my way to my bathroom, I brush my teeth and get ready for bed, my mind reeling with thoughts of the past, the present, and Maddie.

Rosalind and I came to Cambria to live with Gran and Grandad from Santa Barbara when we were teenagers after our parents were killed in a car accident. The loss of our parents still feels painful and often feels as fresh as it did the day it happened. Other than that experience, we've led a happy, full life.

As a thirteen-year-old, I hadn't seen much before my world turned upside down, and thankfully, I hadn't seen too much more since then. After high school, I commuted to college in San Luis Obispo, just like Rosalind is doing now, and got a business degree. Ever since I was a teenager, my life has always centered around this town and my grandparents. They saved me, and I'm grateful to them. Plus, Cambria is comfortable and easy.

So, I stayed and bought the shop. I moved out of their bed and breakfast and into this apartment—my independence.

My grandparents always worry I stay only because of them; they're afraid it's holding me back from finding happiness. And no matter what I say, they worry I'm not being honest with them or with myself.

I understand two things about myself—I'm confident in who I am, and I trust myself.

It's something Gran and Grandad taught me. When you lose your parents at a young age, life can go in different directions. But Ros and I had stability and love. We had encouragement and support. By the time I was a teenager, I knew what I wanted and what was important to me.

In high school and college, I had plenty of friends; if I wanted, I could've had plenty of girls. I didn't want to settle for anything less than what felt right.

My college girlfriend, Lucy, was as close as I came to finding something real. Then, one day, she asked for a little more commitment, and I hesitated. I recognized my hesitation and spoke more truth about where we were headed in our relationship than I considered before that little push. We decided maybe we weren't on the same page after all.

That day, I promised I would never be too casual with another person's feelings or my own. If there were any hesitation, I would be careful to be intentional about what I was starting with that person.

Climbing into bed, I lie on my back, staring at the ceiling.

Every conversation thought, and encounter I've had with Maddie since we met has been with intention, and there hasn't been a single moment of hesitation.

As my eyes close, I allow myself to start dreaming of something new. Something I've never dared to dream.

CHAPTER 11

Ryder

With a unique white chocolate mocha chai that I picked up from Dream Bean Café, I make my way up to Gran and Grandad's back door. Molly told me it's our newest resident's favorite.

Last night, I told Maddie we would talk today, although I'm unsure if first thing in the morning was what either of us envisioned. The first drop-off this morning at the shop isn't until nine, so I decided I want to talk now.

Walking into the house, I hear voices from the kitchen, so I head in that direction. I find Gran, Rosalind, and Maddie sitting around the table when I enter. They all look in my direction in surprise. "Ryder Evans, since when have you visited this early in the morning on a weekday?" Gran asks. My eyes are glued to Maddie, and she looks right back at me.

"Since you hired a charming and beautiful Texan, Gran," Rosalind answers before I even have a chance to speak. Maddie's attention shifts to Ros, but I keep watching her. From the corner of my eye, I see Gran looking at me, a small smile appearing on her face. "Well, is that so," she says.

Now, Maddie's gaze bounces between my sister, Gran, and me as if she isn't sure exactly where this conversation is headed. "Yes, that's so," I respond. "And I brought her new favorite drink, according to Molly Miller, to soften her to my charms since I plan on asking her to dinner on Friday night."

Maddie blushed when I walked closer and set the drink in front of her.

"I knew you were smitten," Ros states.

Gran stands, walks up to me, and raises on her toes to place a kiss on my cheek. "Lovely to see you in the morning, Ryder," she starts walking away, saying, "Rosalind, let's mind our business and get the rest of the morning list done before we need to serve breakfast." Rosalind groans and follows behind her, giving me a smile and a wink before she disappears.

I immediately reach for Maddie's hand, pulling her out of the chair and into me. She comes willingly.

"Good morning," I say.

"Good morning," she whispers back.

I dip my head to look into her eyes before gently resting my lips against hers. I allow my lips to linger on hers with only a little pressure, savoring their connection without taking more. Maddie seems to understand I want to stay in the moment a little longer.

We both pull back eventually, releasing a quiet sigh

and placing our foreheads against one another.

"That was nice," Maddie says.

"I couldn't agree more."

Pulling back, I look down at her. "I know you must get to work, but I had to see you. I won't take up too much time."

"I'm glad you came, but I should probably get moving. It's a check-out day for several guests, after all."

"Then I will make this quick," I tell her. "Will Friday night work for dinner?"

"Yes, I can't think of a better way to spend a Friday night," she says. The smile widened across her face and matched the one on mine.

"I plan on making sure of that," I tell her. "Now, I'm going to leave so you can get to work before Gran comes in here and reprimands me for bothering her employee."

She laughs, and I love the sound. I make a mental note to give her a reason to laugh as much as possible.

"Have a good day, and thank you so much for thinking of me this morning," she says as she picks up the cup of chai, raising it to me in gesture.

"I haven't stopped thinking of you since I saw you blazing around the corner of the cottage, ready to read me the riot act your first morning in town," I share with her over my shoulder as I walk out. I imagine her cheeks just turned the perfect shade of pink. When I reach the doorway between the hall and the kitchen, I turn back and see she's more perfect than I imagined. "Have a good day, Maddie."

Turning on my heels, I leave her standing as pretty as a picture in my grandparents' kitchen, my heart beating at a little quicker pace than it was a week ago.

• • •

When I return to the shop, Sam and Billy are already getting things ready for the day.

"Hey, Boss," Billy says in greeting.

"Good morning," I respond, going over the computer to review the workload for the day. "Mrs. Turner is coming in this morning; she thinks her transmission might go out. Then we have two other more minor issues coming in around one o'clock and three o'clock this afternoon."

"Cool, I'm ready for it," Billy says.

"By the way, how was closing up by yourself? Any questions or concerns?"

"It was totally fine. Everything was smooth and easy. Thanks for trusting me."

"You've earned it. Sam and I appreciate your dependability. Keep it up." I tell him.

Sam comes into the office from the bay. "Hey, dude. I noticed you weren't parked back when I arrived this morning. Anything interesting to share?" He opens a box of donuts that one of them must have picked up on their way in this morning and lifts it in my direction in a silent offer. I wave him off, and he shrugs before pulling a glazed one out.

"Not yet," I state simply. I look over at my best friend and shake my head. He's permanently moved to the beat of his drum. He lacks commitment in all areas of his life except for when it comes to friendships, his parents, and this shop.

He looks up at me, eats half of the donut in one bite, and with his mouth full, says, "Don't believe you, especially since Mom told me that Gayle Rogers told her she saw you at Dream Bean with some pretty girl the other night. And that it was the girl working for your grandparents." He stuffs the rest of the donut in his mouth and walks away.

"You sound like a town hen, dude," I shout after him, laughing.

The bell dings, indicating a customer has pulled up, most likely Mrs. Turner. It's time to start our day, and the quicker this day goes by, the faster I can get through three more workdays to get to Friday night and dinner with Maddie.

Until then, I need to figure out how to focus on work instead of the woman who opened the door to my heart.

CHAPTER 12

Maddie

I got through the workday floating around on cloud nine. Rosalind held her tongue most of the day about what transpired between me and her brother. Evelyn never said a word, as if Ryder showing up to see me this morning was something she anticipated happening.

We were busy with check-ins and check-outs up to three o'clock. The last couple of hours were spent organizing the menu selections and activities each new guest chose during their stay.

One thing I've learned since arriving two weeks ago is organization is critical.

As we started winding down our day, I looked up from the menu I was working on to find Rosalind watching me.

When our eyes meet, she takes it as permission to speak. "Ryder doesn't do things like he did this morning." She states it in such a matter-of-fact way that it almost feels like she's accusing me of something.

"Oh, I…" I begin to say but trail off because I don't know how to respond.

She sighs. I recognize that I'm nervous and don't know what to say. "I'm just stating a fact. It's nothing against you." She shrugs, then continues, "I just wanted you to know because I know what girls think they see when they look at him."

"What do girls think when they see him?" I ask, generally curious.

"They see a handsome guy with charm yet is single and never commits."

"Well, I can agree he is handsome; that is hard to ignore, but I don't know about his dating history. I make no assumptions."

She makes a slightly disgusted face. "I know I just said that is how girls see him, but it still grosses me out a little." We both give each other a knowing smile. "I just wanted you to know that there's more to him than what he lets people see, so if he was here this morning, something has changed. I can only assume that something is you."

I watch her briefly, and she stares back. Neither of us says a word. "Well, don't worry. I'm not the type to take the gesture he made lightly."

"Good," she slides her chair back from the table. "Well, I need to get home to study because I have an exam tomorrow in my economics class. See you Friday."

"Good luck," I call out as she walks away.

She turns back to me, smiling, "Thanks."

Just before she reaches the door, I stop her. "Hey, Ros, one more thing," I say.

"Yeah?" she responds and waits for me to continue.

"Do you think you can give me Ryder's phone number?"

She snickers and shakes her head as she walks back over to the table, grabbing a pen and paper and jotting down what I assume is Ryder's number. She hands it to me and then turns away. "Bye, Maddie," she states before disappearing from the room.

When I look down at the piece of paper she wrote on, I read a phone number, and just above it is the word "lover's."

Once again, I find myself grinning.

• • •

I'd be lying if I said I wasn't expecting—hoping for Ryder to show up tonight. I couldn't help; he has set a precedent for popping in. But he didn't, and that's fine.

It's nine-thirty at night, and I find myself typing, deleting, and then retyping the same two sentences in a text message to Ryder.

> Me: Hi, this is Maddie. Thanks again for the drink this morning.

Sitting on the couch, I curl my feet underneath me and debate, hitting send for the millionth time in the last hour. Finally, I take a deep breath and tap the send button, immediately tossing my phone to the other end of the couch.

Picking up my tea and taking a sip, I wait to hear the sound of a new message arriving. What is wrong with me?

I'm acting nervous, which is silly.

My mind drifts off into deep thought. What is my life right now? It all seems to be moving simultaneously in fast forward and slow motion. God is definitely sending me a gentle reminder that I can plan all I want, but some things are just not in my power.

Saying yes to this date with Ryder on Friday night was in my power and a big step for me, even if it appears to be a small, ordinary action. Boy meets girl. Girl and boy like one another. Boy asks girl on a date. The girl says yes. Yet, while it feels lovely and exciting, I'm also full of trepidation about whether I'm ready.

I find myself considering what Caroline might say. I'm confident she would say, *quit overthinking Madds and enjoy yourself. If it feels right, it's right, and no one, including yourself, should question it.* Of course, I recognize this when I allow myself some grace.

When it comes to Ryder Evans, strangely, in the short time I've known him, it doesn't feel awkward or forced. It's natural, hopeful, comforting, and everything I want in a relationship.

Maybe I shouldn't jump the gun and allow whatever this is to become what it's supposed to be. I need to quit overthinking things and have some fun.

A chime comes from the other end of the couch, indicating I have a message. Of course, it could be from anyone, but I'm pretty sure it's Ryder. I reach across the couch, turning my phone over to find the text message I was waiting for. After putting my code in to open the phone, I tap on the message.

Ryder: Hey, I was thinking about you. I'm glad you tracked down my number. <3

And you're welcome.

Me: ☺ I thought having your number before our date might be a good idea, so I asked Rosalind for it. I'm glad you don't mind.

I want to tell him I was thinking of him, too, but I hesitate. Should I, or shouldn't I?

Me: I was thinking of you, too. How was your day?

Only seconds pass before he replies.

Ryder: It was pretty good. Busy, which I can't ever complain about since it's my livelihood. How was yours?

Me: Good attitude to have... ☺ We were pretty busy with the changeover, but your sister, Gran, and I work well together. I'm so glad I decided to come here.

Ryder: So am I.

It's a good thing he isn't here because he would be able to see the blush that crept across my cheeks.

Ryder: I know you meant because of the bed and breakfast, but I'm still glad.

Be bold, Maddie, I think to myself.

Me: It's not just because of the job. Nothing is what I anticipated when I planned this new chapter. It's more. It's better.

Ryder: I can promise you that you are nothing I could've anticipated.

Blushing again, I sigh. *Dear God, please let Ryder be everything he seems to be.*

Me: I hope that's a good thing.

Ryder: It's better.

I hate to text and run, but I need to get some sleep because I have to drive into San Luis Obispo tomorrow for some parts and other supplies. I'll be gone most of the day, so if we don't talk, I will get in touch Friday morning.

Me: We have a long day, too. Safe travels.

And Ryder, I can't wait for Friday night.

Ryder: Me too.

Goodnight, Maddie. Sweet dreams.

Me: Goodnight. Sweet dreams to you, too.

Whatever happens between us, there isn't a doubt that I want it. I fold the blanket on the couch and make my way to bed. I'm sure if I dream of Ryder, then I will have no problem having sweet dreams.

CHAPTER 13

Ryder

I've only spoken to Maddie briefly since Wednesday to confirm I would pick her up at six o'clock tonight. Otherwise, there has been only the occasional text message for the past day and a half.

I'm missing her. I feel anxious about missing out on any time with her. Friday couldn't get here fast enough, and now it's dragging on like the end of a terrible movie.

When we finished up with the final customer of the day, I ran upstairs to my apartment to shower and change.

Now, as I pull into a driveway I've gone down hundreds or more times in my life, I feel something I've never felt before. Nervous. Excited. Hopeful. It all feels new because of her. Maddie.

I put my truck in park in front of the cottage, hop out, and make my way to the front door. Before I can even knock, the door swings open. Maddie is smiling brightly to greet me.

"Well, hello," I say, returning her grin with my own.

Tucking a loose strand of hair behind her ear, she says, "Hello."

"You ready? You may need a sweater or light jacket."

Holding her finger up for me to wait, she grabs a cream-colored sweater from the back of the couch before turning back to me. "Got it. Now I'm ready."

"Great, let's get going," I say, stepping to the side to allow her to pass.

When we got to my truck, I rushed to open the door for her. It earns me another one of her million-dollar smiles, something I plan to see as often as possible. Once she settles in, I close her door and climb into the driver's seat.

"So, do I get to know where we're going yet?"

"It's a place down in Morro Bay, so we have a little bit of a drive, but it will be worth it."

"Sounds nice. I've never been to Morro Bay. Evelyn and Hank told me about it the other day while we ate lunch."

"It's a nice drive. Let's be honest, pretty much the entire Highway 1 is beautiful," I say. "I will have to show you my favorite spots along the coast."

"I would love that."

"Me too." I pause at the end of the driveway to ensure no one is coming before pulling out and heading toward our destination.

Maddie and I share a comfortable silence as we pass through town. I watch her from the corner of my eyes; her lips turn softly as she looks out the window. She looks so content and relaxed.

My eyes drift back to the road before me, and I feel the same contentment.

• • •

Maddie

From the moment I opened the door when Ryder arrived to pick me up, I was excited about what this night might hold. Sure, I'm nervous, but only because it's been years since I've been out on a first date.

As we drive through Cambria, I can't help taking it in with a new perspective. It's different from the one I had a few weeks ago when I arrived. It's amazing all that has changed in such a short time. There are some changes I wasn't anticipating, but they're welcome ones. And changes I was hoping for, like the peaceful, calming feeling that I made the right decision to move here.

We turn onto Highway 1, and I see a mileage sign with Pismo Beach on it.

I keep my eyes staring out the passenger side window, and we reach a point where I can see the ocean all the way to the horizon's edge. It's breathtaking—a beauty to be admired and appreciated.

As my mind drifts to all the possibilities of life that the vastness of the ocean can represent, I suddenly feel a warm, calloused hand take mine and intertwine with my fingers. When I looked at him, his eyes were on the road, and he did not indicate that he felt the electricity pass between us as I did. A sort of fiery sensation, one I'm sure I could never get enough of.

"This is okay, right?" he asks, nodding toward our intertwined hands.

"It's perfect."

"You're perfect," he responds, never taking his eyes off the road ahead. I squeeze his hand in response, and he gently squeezes back.

I thought I'd seen the best part of the drive, but nothing prepared me for what I saw as we came around a curve at the top of a hill. Before us, I can see for miles and miles. I can see an oceanside town below, the ocean dwarfing its size with its enormity.

I don't even realize the gasp that escapes between my lips at the sight of it, and this time, Ryder squeezes my hand. "It's indescribable, isn't it?"

"It's incredible," I say.

He gives me a knowing smile. I take it all in, and he gives me the space to. We've already spent most of the drive in silence, which leaves me speechless.

I have an appreciation for nature and all the beauty it can hold. Texas has so much natural beauty in its flatlands, mountainous desert, and even its rolling hills with lakes and rivers running through them. It's beautiful and captivating. But this is different. Not better and definitely not worse. Just different. I can see and appreciate it all.

People are that way, too. Full of differences and similarities, but all worth being in complete awe of.

My gaze moves to Ryder. It's funny how you can meet someone, and your whole view on life can change quickly.

Become something different. And while your past had its beauty, this new view holds something fascinating, worthy, and in his words…indescribable.

CHAPTER 14

Ryder

I've watched Maddie the entire drive into Morro Bay. I noticed how her eyes lit up when we saw the horizon across the Pacific Ocean. I felt the excitement in the tiny gasp that slipped out when we came around the curve at the top of the hill overlooking the coastline of Morro Bay.

It's something I've seen my whole life. A view I've experienced thousands of times before, yet this time was different. Like I was seeing it for the first time. And it was spectacular to witness. I let her take it all in and only talked when she spoke to me.

Even as we drove into the town of Morro Bay, her eyes darted from place to place. It was as if she were afraid she would miss something. It was like every little town along the coast, no different than Cambria. It makes me wonder about the world she comes from and what the places within it look like.

As we got closer to the restaurant, I hated to interrupt this moment, but my curiosity got the best of me. "Does this look different than where you're from? Aside from the obvious enormous ocean looming on one side of us along the highway?"

She turns her attention from the scenery to me. "Yeah, there's something different in the way things are laid out, in the colors of the buildings, and differences in architecture. They're subtle differences, and I think it's interesting that when you grow up in one area, you assume everything looks the same everywhere. I mean, sure, I've watched movies set in other places, but most likely, I was concentrating on the movie itself and not as much on the specifics of the setting." She smiles and looks out the window again. "I mean, I knew everything wasn't the same, but it's different when you see it in person."

"Don't you remember coming to Cambria when you were a kid? You saw the ocean then," I say.

"Well, yeah, but we didn't come this way, and I guess I just wasn't mindful of the details I'm noticing now, ya know?"

"Yeah, that makes sense," I tell her.

We pull up to The Galley Seafood Grill & Bar, a casual waterfront restaurant I've visited since I was a kid. "Here we are," I say. Unbuckling my seat belt, I tell her, "Don't move." I hop out and rush around to the passenger side of the truck.

When I open her door, she has a wide grin across her face. "Thank you, sir," she says when I offer her my hand to help her step out of the truck. When our hands meet, I feel that same sensation I've felt every time I've touched her. I can't find my voice, so I smile in response.

She doesn't release my hand even after she's out of the truck. I don't let go of hers either.

We walk hand in hand into the restaurant, and once inside, we're greeted by the hostess, a young girl named Jenny, according to her nametag. I let her know we have a reservation and give her my name while Maddie stands quietly beside me.

As the young hostess leads us to our table, Maddie whispers, "This place looks so sweet."

Sweet? Her Southern charm pours from her. I've never heard anyone describe a restaurant as sweet, but I like it. She's right, too. This place has always had a warm, comfortable feel to it.

Maddie is different than any other person I've met in my life. And I can't wait to find out what makes her so unique.

Jenny led us to one of the tables, lining the windows looking out over the water. "Will this be okay for you?" she asks. I look at Maddie, and she nods her agreement. "Perfect," I say, looking back at Jenny.

While she places the menus on the table, I pull a chair out for Maddie to sit first. She happily takes a seat. "Your multiple acts of chivalry have been noted, and I appreciate them," she says. I can't see her face, but I can hear the grin in her voice.

As I walk around the table to take my seat, I say, "It's the one thing that stuck out in my mind that my dad always did for my mom. He always opened doors for her, pulled her chair out, and even held the umbrella over her on rainy days." I smile at the memories. My dad always respected my mom, and she loved him even more for it. It didn't matter how young I was; I recognized it in how they looked at each other. And I knew it was the one thing I wanted for myself one day: a woman I loved that way and one who loved me the same.

"My dad has always done the same for my mom," she tells me. "He taught my brothers to be gentlemen, and he ensured my sister, and I always appreciated the gesture behind it. It isn't something I always see, but I like it." I watch her facial features change, with each memory rolling through her mind as she speaks. Interestingly, if you pay close enough attention to the story beyond the words spoken, you might learn something about a person. Maddie loves her family.

She sighs, then picks up her menu. "So, what's good here?" she asks me, her eyes roaming the pages before her. She makes a humming sound as she reads each item.

I open my menu and begin to glance over it, knowing good and well that I always get one of two things. "Well, I tend to order the fish and chips or the scallops. It just depends on how fancy I'm feeling," I smile.

A burst of laughter comes from across the table. When I look up, she's shaking her head, her eyes on me while she giggles. "How fancy you feel, huh?"

My grin grows wider. Man, she's cute. "Yep."

"Well, I'm not really the fancy type," she tells me as her giggles finally subside.

"Good because I'm craving the fish and chips tonight,"

I say, closing my menu.

Maddie closes her menu, too, laying it down on the table in front of her and resting her hands on top of it. Her gaze lifts to mine, a massive grin on her face, and she says, "It's settled. If you're not fancy tonight, then I'm not fancy tonight. I'll have the same."

It's my turn to laugh. Maddie isn't like any girl I've met. She's charming, funny, and down to earth. I've never felt more comfortable or at ease. She sits across the table from me, smiling, solidifying that she possesses all those qualities and is the most beautiful woman I've met. Our gazes lock, my laughter subsides, and her smile changes slightly. Not a frown. Something positive and hopeful. I've tried to tell myself this attraction to Maddie means nothing more than a physical attraction. But I'm just lying to myself. I begin to say something but don't know what to say. Before the words can form, our waitress walks up. Her name is Beth.

"I see your menus are down. What can I get the two of you?" Beth asks.

"Oh, uh…I'll have the fish and chips," Maddie responds, handing her menu to Beth.

Beth's attention turns to me, "And for you?"

"I'll have the same," I tell her.

"Great, two fish and chips," Beth says as she jots it down on her pad. "Anything to drink?"

"I'll take a Woodford's on the rocks and some water," I tell her. We both look over at Maddie and wait for her reply. "Why change things now? I'll have one, too," she says, as she keeps her focus on me. And there it is, that ease. That comfort. The way she makes it so simple to become enamored of her without even meaning to.

Beth nods her head, "You got it." She turned and walked away, leaving Maddie and me alone again.

Maddie fidgets with her napkin, her gaze roaming around the restaurant and out the window.

"Tell me about you and your life before you moved half away across the country," I say, breaking the silence.

Her gaze refocuses on me. I wait, returning her regard. She seems to relax again. "Well, I grew up in a small, one-stoplight town in the Texas Hill Country. I have an older brother and sister. Family is everything to me. Once I graduated from high school, I went to college close to home. Other than the rare vacation with my grandparents, I never went too far from home. Until now." Maddie says all of this in practically one breath. She starts fidgeting with her napkin again.

"What changed?" I feel compelled to ask.

She looks up again. "Everything, really. I guess life happened. Real life. The warm little bubble I lived in burst, and I felt like I was drowning." She pauses, and her gaze turns to the ocean beyond the window. "I was the cliché small-town girl. I fell in love young with the boy next door. I spent the better half of my life believing I would marry him, have kids and pets, and live in that same little town for the rest of my life. I was content with being with the same man for the rest of my life. Unfortunately, Connor started turning the pages of his life in a new book." Maddie gives me a sad, half smile. "And I decided it was time to write my own story."

I'm not sure what to say. Her heart was broken, and I understand that more than she knows. "I'm glad you chose Cambria to find this new life story."

When our eyes meet again, Maddie gives me a small smile. "Me, too."

It's strange to realize how two little words can make you feel so much.

CHAPTER 15

Maddie

Leaning back in my chair, I rub my full belly. "Ugh, I'm stuffed like a little pig." Ryder sits across from me with a wide grin as he puts another bite of dessert in his mouth. "Where are you putting all of that?" I ask.

His smile widens, and his cheeks puff out like a squirrel storing up for winter. Ryder mumbles through his full mouth, "The res…eve…tank."

I can't help but laugh, and the jiggling of my belly causes me to groan, "Ughhhh, don't make me laugh."

He swallows hard and says, "I told you that you didn't need to eat all your food." The expression on his face is teasing and adorable.

"Yeah, you did, but I have no willpower when it comes to good food," I tell him.

Our entire dinner has gone just as easy as this conversation. There was only a brief awkwardness at the beginning, and that was only because we both felt like whatever was happening between us had nearly pulled the rug from beneath our feet.

While everything feels so good and easy when I'm with him, Ryder causes my insides to feel like I'm on one of those loopy-loop roller coasters. Exciting. Happy. And completely scared, all at the same time.

He leans back in his chair, almost mirroring my posture, "Apparently, neither do I." He gives me a wink, and I feel like I'm melting. And there is that warm, fluttery feeling again.

Thank God for Beth, our waitress, because if she hadn't just walked up, I surely would've said something in return to embarrass myself.

"How are things going over here?" Beth looks between me and Ryder with a sweet smile.

"Good…amazing…" I begin to say, and Ryder interrupts me before I can complete my response.

"Amazingly full," he finishes.

Beth cracks up, "You both did an outstanding job finishing your food. Any mother out there would be proud."

This time, it's mine and Ryder's turn to laugh. We both rest a hand on our stomachs, trying to hold our stomachs from moving around too much.

"I'll get these plates out of your way. Are you ready for the check?" she asks.

"That would be great," Ryder replies.

After Beth grabs our empty dishes from the table and walks away, Ryder reaches across the table and takes my hand as I'm wiping up some water from the table. He took it between his hands and gently caressed my palm with his thumb. "So, are you ready to head home, or would you like to take a short walk on the beach?

"The beach sounds lovely. Maybe we can walk off some of these calories we just consumed," I say.

Beth is back and places the check down in front of Ryder. We both look up, and he releases my hand. "Thank you both so much. I hope you enjoy the rest of your night, and please come back in soon."

We both say in unison, "Thank you."

"Everything was great," Ryder continues.

Ryder pulled his wallet out and put some cash on the check tray before standing and extending his hand to me. "Shall we?"

Looking up into his eyes, I nod. "We shall."

We walk hand in hand through the restaurant and out the doors. The evening air is cool, and a shiver runs through my body. "You cold?" Ryder asks.

"I'm good; the initial feeling was just surprising. My body needed to adjust."

"Got it." He led me around the side of the restaurant until we saw a small beach in front of us, the waves crashing against the shore and a slight breeze swirling around us. Another shiver runs up my arms, "Okay, yep. I'm cold," I say, laughing.

"Do you want to go?" he asks.

"Nope." I turn to him, and wrapping my arms around his waist, I look up to find him looking down at me. "I'll just stay right here if that's okay?"

Pulling me tighter to him and placing his arms around

me, he says, "There's nothing more okay than this." His lips begin to lower toward mine, and I rise on my toes to meet him halfway. When our lips meet, there is an electric response that's both shocking and welcomed. Ryder's mouth softly caressed mine, and we moved together, savoring this feeling between us. Then, something switched like it did the first time we kissed; a fire engulfed my entire body, encouraging me to deepen the kiss and pull him closer. It feels like I can't get close enough. Ryder's emotions seem to match mine, his tongue sliding along my lips and tangling with mine.

I can't remember if I was cold before because this kiss has warmed every inch of my body.

Our kiss begins to slow, and Ryder places his lips tenderly against mine one final time before pulling back. "Let's get out of here before things get out of hand," he says.

Nodding, I lay my head against his chest and squeeze him tightly, still wanting more. Ryder doesn't pull away; he reciprocates my touch.

After a few seconds, he pulled back and took my hand, "Come on."

We stroll back to his truck in comfortable silence. Ryder opened the door for me and waited for me to climb into the passenger side before he shut the door and walked around. I watch him, and it suddenly hits me. Happiness. I'm so happy and have no idea what's next, but I'm okay with that because I haven't felt this way in a long time. I know that Ryder Evans is a massive part of this new feeling.

CHAPTER 16

Ryder

The conversation was effortless on our drive back to Cambria. We laughed, shared childhood stories, and continued to learn about each other.

When I make the last turn to her cottage, a comfortable silence falls between us, so I reach over and take Maddie's hand. She doesn't pull away. She only glances over to me as a sweet smile spreads across her lips, and she clasps my hand a little tighter. Her gaze returns to the road in front of us.

As we pull into the driveway and make our way down to her home, I tell her, "This was one of the best nights I've had in a long time."

"Me too. It's been so long. Longer than I can recall," she replies. Maddie gets a sort of faraway look on her face, and she stares out the window across the back lawn.

Pulling to a stop, I shut the engine off, which draws Maddie's attention in my direction. "So…" I say.

"So," she returns. Maddie unfastened her seatbelt and leaned across the truck's center console toward me. I reach for her, taking her face between my hands and bringing our lips together. The moment our lips collide, that out-of-control feeling picks up exactly where we left off on the beach in Morro Bay. Kissing Maddie feels like playing with a match; the only outcome is catching fire completely. My mind gets clouded by desire, and the moment I hear a moan leave her, we both try pulling one another closer. The problem is there's not enough room for us to get as close as we want. As close as I need. She begins climbing over the console, and a loud bang echoes through the truck. "Owww, shoot," she yelps, pulling back from me.

"Shit, you okay?" I ask.

Rubbing her knee, she sits back into the passenger side seat. We both look at one another and burst out laughing. "I'm sorry," I say between bouts of laughter.

"No, I'm sorry," she says. "I'm such a klutz."

We both continue laughing. "In your defense, this is a bit of a confined space for all these feelings," I tell her.

As our laughter subsides, I reluctantly say, "I think that's a sign I should walk you to your door and say good-night. Wait right there, don't move."

Before she responds, I hop out of the truck, running around to the other side to help her. When I pull the door open, Maddie is grinning.

"Allow me," I say, reaching my hand out for her to take so I can help her out of the truck. Maddie doesn't hesitate to accept my offer. We remain hand in hand after she steps out of the truck.

We make our way over to the front porch, and when we reach the door, we stop and face one another. "Maddie, this night has been amazing," I tell her.

Her eyes light up, and she nods, "You have been the perfect gentleman. Thank you."

"And I plan on continuing to be just that..." I say, leaning forward and placing a kiss on her cheek. "Goodnight, Madelyn." Her eyes are shut when I pull back, and a soft sigh escapes her lips.

"Goodnight, Ryder."

Stepping back from her and leaving Maddie watching me at the door, I force myself to turn around and get into my truck.

I quickly crank the engine before I change my mind and watch Maddie enter the cottage, glancing back over her shoulder and giving me a tiny wave before the door closes.

My body, heart, and mind are at war. I want to turn off this truck, knock on her door, and stay with her. The right thing to do—the gentlemanly thing to do—is to go home to my bed and call her tomorrow.

And that's precisely what I do. I drive home and wonder the entire way just how much longer I can be a gentleman. Everything in me tells me that Maddie is special; greedily, I want more.

• • •

Madelyn Jennings was the last thing on my mind when I finally fell asleep last night, and she was the first thing on my mind this morning. I reach over to my bedside table and grab my phone.

Scrolling through my text messages, I tap Maddie's name and start typing her a text.

> Me: Good morning. Thanks again for last night. I should be getting off around noon today. Can you have lunch today? I can come to you. Lunch in hand.

Setting my phone back down, I toss the comforter off and roll out of bed. I stretch my arms high above my head to get my blood flowing before grabbing my towel for a quick shower.

I turn the knob of the shower as far over as I can in hopes that the water will get hot quickly. I touch the stream of water to check the temperature, and just before I step in, I hear a chime from my phone. I smile, knowing it's most likely a text from Maddie.

Taking the quickest shower of my life, I step out and dry off in record time. I wrap the towel around my waist and head straight to my phone.

Just as I hoped, it was Maddie. I swipe up to read the text.

> Maddie: Good morning to you, too. I should be the one saying thank you for last night. Thank you for the delicious meal and for having enough of a level head about you to remain a gentleman till the end. You have no idea how much that means to me. That being said, lunch would be fantastic. We only have one check-in today so that I won't

be working a full day.

I quickly respond.

> Me: Being a gentleman wasn't easy. I didn't want to leave you.

I imagine Maddie reading that and blushing.

> Maddie: ☺ Being a lady wasn't easy for me, so we're even there. I didn't want you to leave me either.
>
> Me: Maddie.

I couldn't bring myself to finish my thought. Being shy isn't something I usually have a problem with, but I guess that's what I'm feeling right now. It's mixed with a bit of fear of everything Maddie makes me feel. It's uncharted territory. My phone chimes with another new message. I'm sure she's confused about why I only sent a text with her name.

> Maddie: Yes, Ryder?
>
> Me: Sorry. I …
>
> Me: Let's talk at lunch. Will 12:30 be okay?

Her response was quick.

> Maddie: Okay, I hope everything is okay. And 12:30 should be perfectly fine. See you later then.

The tone of her text changed. She seems a little worried, and I feel bad because I know it's because I said we would talk later. I need to reassure her that things couldn't be better.

Me: Everything is more than okay, Maddie. I promise.
12:30 it is. I can't wait to see you.

Hopefully, she gets the feeling behind my text. Seeing her is all I will be thinking about from now until lunch.

Maddie: Great, I agree. Have a good morning. See you. ☺

I read her text with a grin, then place it on the bedside table while I get dressed.

It's seven forty-five, and I need to open the shop in fifteen minutes. I'm definitely behind my regular schedule. I grab my phone and keys and head out the door.

Four hours and forty-two minutes until I see Maddie again. *It's going to be a long morning*, I think as I lock the door of my apartment.

CHAPTER 17

Maddie

I read Ryder's text multiple times throughout the morning. *Everything is more than okay, Maddie. I promise.*

This sounds like a good thing. Initially, I was a little worried when he didn't finish his text, but he obviously had something to say. His something is good. Yes. His something is undoubtedly good, so I will stop obsessing over it immediately.

T- minus thirty minutes until Ryder is supposed to be here.

I'm tidying up my desk when I hear someone from behind. As I turn around, I catch a glimpse of Ros leaning against the doorway, watching me.

When we make eye contact, she slowly says, "You had a date with my brother, huh?"

"Well, yes. Is that okay?" I ask.

I'm trying to read her face and figure out what she's thinking, but if I've learned anything about Ros over the last month, she is hard to read. Not to mention, it wasn't too long ago she questioned me about Ryde and my intentions. It almost seemed like she was warning me last time. But this time, she seems to have a different mission.

She takes a step toward me with a serious look on her face. I resist the urge to step back. I almost laugh at how protective Ros is over Ryder. It's such a sweet sisterly gesture.

"That depends," she says, taking another step until she is standing close to me.

"Umm, okay," I croak. Her demeanor stays serious, and she remains silent. "And what does it depend upon?"

"It depends on whether you're just passing through or if you can see yourself staying here for a while at least," she says. I can see genuine concern on her face with a closer look. She's being protective now. It's sweet, and honestly, Ros is a little scary when she's being protective.

"I have no plans of leaving any time soon. And if I'm honest, although it's been only a month, Ryder makes me think less of leaving and more of staying than I thought possible."

Rosalind pulls me into a quick hug before I know what is happening. Once it registers in my mind, I reciprocate the affection. She pulls back, and there's a wide grin on her face now.

"Good, because I think Ryder really likes you. I told you before he doesn't do things like this, show his feelings, commit, so I wanted to be certain." She shrugs. "I just happen to like you, too."

I can't help but return the smile. "I like you, too. As

for Ryder, I like him, and that's both exciting and scary. I promise you, it's not my intention to hurt him."

She gives me a slight wave of the hand. "I wasn't apprehensive about you hurting Ryder. He's a big boy, but I feel like he's acting differently with you than anyone else."

I'm hearing what Ros is saying, but I'm not sure of the meaning behind her words.

"I don't follow."

Shrugging, she says, "Ryder has had one person who ever captured his attention, and even then, she wanted more than he wanted to give. But, with you, he seems more in tune." Again, Ros shrugs her shoulders, "I don't know. Ignore me. It's just a feeling I get whenever I see him around you. The other day in the kitchen is a prime example. It's like you're the only person in the room."

I take in what she says, plus Ryder's text from this morning. I don't know if I believe he is as taken with me as Ros thinks, but it makes me wonder exactly what I feel for him.

"Anyway, maybe I should've just said I hope you had a good time last night and left it at that," she tells me. "But I didn't, so let's just put it on the record that I hope this thing between you two is exactly what you hope it will be."

And in true Ros fashion, she turned and left me alone in my office, wondering what I was hoping for.

• • •

When I walk out of the back door, there's a slight breeze, but the sun is shining through the trees and across the expanse of the backyard. It's nearly twelve-thirty, and the anticipation of seeing Ryder creates a nervous energy in the pit of my stomach.

Walking closer to my house, I see Ryder sitting on the front porch. I wonder how long he's been waiting for me. There's a smile on his face, and as I get closer, it begins to spread. Instantly, the nervous feeling I had a few moments ago has turned into something else—overwhelming joy.

He stands up and begins walking forward, so I pick up my pace. Now, my grin is matching the one on his face. When only a few feet separate us, he says, "Hi."

"Hi," I respond.

Suddenly, I'm in his arms, and his mouth is pressed firmly against mine. I instantly respond by wrapping my arms around his waist and kissing him right back. It's brief but intense. Ryder pulls back, looks me in the eyes, and says, "Twelve thirty couldn't get here quick enough."

"My feelings exactly," I say.

He smiles. "Are you hungry?"

"Starving," I say. "I haven't eaten all day."

"Great." Taking me by the hand, he leads me back to my front porch, only stopping to grab the blanket on the rocker and the bag holding our lunch. Ryder immediately turns back to the yard and guides me to one of the large, shaded trees that fill the lawn. He seems to know what he's doing, so I don't say anything. I only watch him, still trying to work out exactly what I want to happen between us. "This spot, okay?" He asks.

"It's perfect," I say. "It's such a beautiful day."

"I know; we couldn't have had a better day for a picnic," he replies.

He lets go of my hand and sets the food bag down before laying out a blanket for us to sit on. We both take a seat across from each other. "I wasn't exactly sure what you would want, so I just picked up a variety of things from the store before I headed over," he explains as he begins pulling out different items from the bag.

"This girl right here is not picky, and I'm so hungry right now I could eat a horse," I say, laughing.

Ryder watches me as I dig into the food without hesitation. I stuff a bite in my mouth, and with my cheeks full, I give him a closed-mouth grin. He busts out laughing, but I continue to enjoy my lunch.

As his laughter subsides, he says, "You're surprising and unlike any other girl I've ever known. I think I could be in danger of falling in love with you."

I freeze mid-bite and look over at him wide-eyed. He glances my way and seems a bit startled. I place my sandwich back down, pick up a water bottle, and take a long, hard swig. "Maddie, I uh... I," he stops briefly. "The thing is, I don't do this. The dating thing, the getting involved, or the commitment thing with anyone. I've been there before, and it just hasn't been something I've wanted to do again."

I begin to say something, but I don't know what to say, "Ryder, I..."

"No, wait, let me finish. The thing is, you're different, and you've changed something in me. I don't understand how or why, but you changed something. Usually, I don't want to try anything unless I'm certain. It's the reason I never have relationships. And even though I have no idea what's happening between us or if I can be certain this will last, I still want it. I want it to last. I want you, and that's all that matters to me."

He sits there watching me, and I know he's waiting for me to say something. But I can only think about how Connor never once said anything like this to me. And Ryder just confirmed that my hope is the same as his for our relationship.

"I'm sorry if I said too much," he says nervously.

"No," I say, reaching my hand out for his. "You didn't say too much at all. You said just the right amount and everything I needed to hear."

Relief washes over his face. "So, now what?"

"I have no idea," I say. "And I'm okay with that. I spent my whole life wanting to know what was next, and the moment I finally let go, you showed up. So, I think we continue the way we are, getting to know one another and enjoying being together."

Ryder leans forward and places his lips softly against mine. There's no urgency, only gentleness as if he's trying to reassure me that we're in this together without using words.

CHAPTER 18

Ryder

As my lips touch hers, I'm not worried about anyone seeing us. Although, one of my grandparents may be watching from the kitchen window or lurking about somewhere else.

Right now, nothing really matters. And I like it. I like that I don't feel entirely in control. Or that I'm not sure what the hell I'm doing or feeling about this girl who blew into town and turned my world into a topsy-turvy in such a short amount of time. Gran always says you don't need much time to know when something feels right.

Being with Maddie feels right.

I pull back from our kiss and find Maddie's eyes closed. She takes a deep breath, her eyes flutter open, and she makes a humming sound. She's so damn beautiful, especially with sunlight moving across her face. "Beautiful," I say aloud.

She looks directly at me and asks, "What?"

"I said, beautiful. You, Madelyn, are beautiful."

"Oh, thank you," she says, seemingly surprised.

She giggles, and I'm a little confused by her reaction. My face must show it because she begins to explain. "My grandmother always told me that if someone compliments me, I should never hesitate to say thank you. It made me laugh because I think this is the first time I've followed her advice. And for a moment, I thought how proud she would be." She continues to smile. "Silly, I know. It's probably just nerves."

"You're nervous?"

"Yeah, a little. I've been out with one guy my entire life, and well, I guess I'm not sure how to do any of this."

"I think you're doing just fine, so don't worry about a thing," I tell her. "Why don't we finish lunch."

Maddie lies back, resting her head on her hands. I pick up my sandwich and watch her. She looks so relaxed and content. I must admit I'm feeling the exact same way.

"Do you think Evelyn and Henry are watching us from the window?"

"If they haven't been already, they will be soon. Are you prepared to answer questions about us? Because they will most likely have a ton of them."

"Sure, that couldn't be nearly as nerve-wracking as being questioned by your sister," Maddie laughs. I look over at her in confusion, but her position hasn't changed. She's still as relaxed as ever, and her comment was perfectly normal.

"Questioned by my sister?"

Maddie turned over on her side and propped her head

on her hand. "Oh yeah, she sort of cornered me in my office just before I left for the day," she says, smiling. "No biggie, Ros was just trying to be a protective sister. She also informed me that she fully approves of us." Her whole demeanor is so carefree. I should be annoyed at Rosalind, but instead, I can only focus on Maddie just calling us an *us*.

"Us. I like the way that sounds," I say. "Do you think this is all too fast?"

She sits up and crosses her legs, then begins to fiddle with a strand of hair falling from her ponytail. I wait for her to say something because I can tell she wants to. "Honestly, I think it's fast, but who's to say it's too fast? I spent eleven years of my life with the same person, and I'm only twenty-six. People used to tell us we were too young to be with the same person for that long, and look how that turned out. Did it turn out that way because we were too young? I don't think so because I know what I felt at that time and at that moment. And I wouldn't change a thing because it made me who I am today." Maddie leans toward me and takes my hand in hers. With her eyes focused on our hands, she intertwines our fingers, gently rubbing her thumb over my skin. "Only you and I can decide what is too fast for us." She looks up at me now. "I'm willing to risk too fast if you are."

"Well, okay then. That settles everything. We have no idea what is happening, but we're doing this anyway," I say.

She squeezes my hand that's still resting in hers. "Yeah, we are," she says with excitement.

"Now that we're done with all that seriousness, why don't we clean this up and talk about where we're going for dinner tonight?"

"How about I cook for you? We can stay in and watch a movie," she suggests.

"I think I like the way that sounds. How about at my place?"

"Perfect! Why don't I get cleaned up quickly? Then we can go to the grocery store and pick up things we need to make dinner. Oh, and run into Dream Bean Cafe for an afternoon treat," she says, waggling her eyebrows at me.

Not only beautiful but cute, too. I think to myself.

"Sounds like a plan. Let's go," I say as I hop off the blanket.

I extend my hand to Maddie to help her up, and she willingly takes it. I pull her up quickly and continue until she's in my arms. She wraps her arms around my shoulders, draping them over me in a loose hug. I lower my mouth to hers for a brief kiss. Man, I don't think I'll ever get tired of kissing her.

"I've got all this," I tell her as I motion to the picnic. "You go get ready. And while you do that, I will run up to the front house and say hello to my grandparents."

"That's very brave of you," she teases.

"Nah, I'm not worried one bit. I'd be more worried if they'd seen me and knew I left without coming in to say hello before sneaking off with you," I say.

"Good point, and very smart of you," she tells me before turning and heading toward her house. "Give me about thirty minutes," she says as she walks away.

I only take my eyes off her once she is through her doorway and out of sight. No one has ever had me wrapped around their finger, but Madelyn Jennings might be the first.

• • •

Walking through the back door of my grandparents' house, I hear whispers from the kitchen. Shaking my head, I smile to myself. I try to make a little more noise with my shoes against the wood floors to give them some warning that I'm walking in. This should be fun.

As I round the corner through the kitchen doorway, I glimpse my grandmother gently swatting my grandfather on the arm. I hold in a laugh so they don't realize they've been caught. When they see me enter the room, they look up and give me awkward smiles. It's getting harder for me to hold in the laughter with these two.

"Oh, hello, Ryder. We didn't know you were stopping by," Gran says in greeting as she busies herself with drying some dishes.

Grandad sat at the table when I walked in, and I joined him.

"Uh...yeah, what brings you by, Ry?" Grandad asks.

Good lord, they are horrible actors. Instead of calling them out for spying on our picnic date, I decide to play along somewhat. I know it's killing them to feel like they have to pretend they aren't curious about what is happening between Maddie and me, so I decided to let the cat out of the bag.

Not to mention, I have no doubt they both had their noses pressed to the window, watching us while we picnicked out back.

"Hey, you two. I brought Maddie a picnic lunch," I say. "We just finished, so I decided to come up and say hello before I head out."

"Oh, that's nice. For Maddie. Lunch. How thoughtful," Gran stutters out.

"Yes, we had a date last night, too," I say.

"Oh," Grandad says nonchalantly.

Is "oh" the only word in their vocabulary they know to pretend all of this isn't intriguing to them? It makes me want to laugh again.

"Yes, I figured you knew about our date last night since Rosalind knew," I say and await their response.

"Ah, yes. I think it may have been mentioned," Gran says.

"Oh," I say with playful sarcasm.

"And…and I believe I saw you pick her up," Grandad adds to the conversation.

"Oh," I say and then decide to tease them a little more. "And did you also watch out the window when I dropped her off?"

"No, I went to bed before you got baaa…" Grandad starts to say, then realizes his slip of the tongue. He quickly looks over at me, and I'm just sitting with my chin resting in my hands, watching him.

"So, you were spying out the window?" I ask.

Gran's been standing at the sink since I walked in and only glances over her shoulder when she says, "We would never spy and invade your privacy."

"Of course not," I return.

"The thing is, I saw you drive up, and well, you're my grandson, so I thought I'd walk around back and greet you. But then I noticed you walking up to Maddie's door and not making your way here. That's all," Grandad explains.

"I see," I say. Then, I decided to cut them some slack because they both looked like I kicked a puppy. "I'm only teasing you both. I came here to let you know that Maddie and I are dating. And I know that might worry you," I say.

Gran walks over and places a hand on my shoulder. "It's not that we're worried, just feeling a little cautious. For the both of you," she says.

"You know, that's funny because I'm not feeling worried or cautious for the first time," I tell them.

"She's a good, sweet girl," Grandad says.

"I know."

"And you're a special young man," Gran says.

"Well, that may be debatable," I tease, and she swats me playfully like I saw her do to my grandfather a few moments ago.

"You know, you two took a liking to one another that week she was visiting with her grandparents all those years ago," Grandad says. "It's no wonder you would do so again."

I look at both of them, a little shocked.

"We met before?" I ask, still in disbelief.

"Yes, dear. I may have something that will trigger your memory," Gran tells me. "I'll be right back."

Maddie and I have met before? What in the hell?

"Found it," I hear her chime from down the hall.

CHAPTER 19

Ryder

After I leave my grandparents, I walk back across the lawn to see if Maddie is ready to go. I must admit, I'm feeling a little bit excited to show her what my grandmother found. I wonder if she remembers because I know I didn't until I saw this blast from the past. I put the picture in my top pocket.

I'm certain she would've said something to me had she remembered we met all those years ago when she was visiting with her grandparents in Cambria.

The door swung open as I stepped up on the porch, and Maddie stepped out.

"Hey, there! You ready?" I ask. When we make eye contact, and I see her, all other thoughts are lost. She's beautiful with a sweet smile on her face, and the best part is it's all for me.

"Yep, ready as I'll ever be," she says.

"Then let's do this," I say as we head for my truck.

I open the passenger door for her and then walk around to my side. I climb into the truck and click on the seat belt. Maddie is watching me like she wants to ask me something.

"What's up? You look like you want to ask me something," I say.

She bites her lower lip before saying, "Well, I'm just wondering if your grandparents said anything about us."

Maddie watches me expectantly. I laugh a little just thinking about Gran and Granddad and how they both tried to play off their curiosity. Maddie's eyebrows shoot up in confusion about why I laughed at her question.

"Why are you laughing?" she asks.

"Sorry, it's just that they both were so awkward trying to pretend like they weren't watching us through the window. It was hilarious. But yes, they did ask if you can call it asking. I think they were just more curious about what was happening between us. They weren't concerned," I pause. "I guess you could say they seemed cautiously happy about it."

I look over at her just as she breathes a quiet sigh of relief.

"Huh, well, I guess that's good. I was a little worried they may think that if we date and something doesn't quite go right, it could affect my job at the bed and breakfast," she says.

The best part about being in a small town is that everything is so close together, and we're already pulling up to the curb outside the grocery store. It's a Saturday, so downtown is a little busy.

"Wait right there. I'll be right there," I tell her.

I practically run around the front of the truck to the passenger side.

As I open the door, I ask, "Have any ideas about what we should make for dinner?"

"Yes, I was thinking I would make my grandmother's meatball recipe with pasta," she tells me. "Does that sound good to you?"

"Sounds delicious," I answer.

We walk into the store hand in hand, moving quickly through the aisles. She seems to have a mental grocery list with every item she needs for the recipe. When we get to the spices, she asks me what I have at my house already, and since it's only salt and pepper, we grab quite a few items.

"Okay, I think that's it," she says.

"Wait, we need one more thing. I can't eat pasta and meatballs without garlic bread," I tell her.

We grab some French bread from the bakery section and then head to the checkout line. Together, we start emptying the basket onto the conveyor belt. "I'll take care of all this."

"No, you treated me to dinner last night," she says.

I place the last item on the belt. "Nope, my house, I pay."

Maddie rolls her eyes at me. "Fine, but our next dinner is at my house, and I pay."

"Deal."

We watch as Betsy, one of the cashiers, scans each item like a pro while the conveyor belt moves everything forward. She's quick, wholly focused on getting us through her line as fast as possible since a line is beginning to form behind us.

Maddie and I help by bagging our groceries.

"Thanks, Betsy," I say as I walk around the end of the checkout to swipe my card through the card reader.

Betsy gives me a warm smile. "No problem, Ryder. Nice to see you both," Betsy says, smiling at me and Maddie. Man, oh, man. The gossip mill will surely be turning. The funny thing is, I don't care.

"You, too," Maddie and I respond in unison, which only causes Betsy to smile brighter.

As we head out the door, I notice several locals eyeing us until we're out of sight. I guess it's big news when Ryder Evans is seen with a woman several times and then even more suspicious when they're seen buying groceries together.

• • •

"This is much bigger than I expected," Maddie says as we walk through the doors of my loft apartment. "And it's very manly yet cozy. I like it."

I watch her as her eyes roam over my apartment while I set the bag of groceries on the kitchen island.

"Thanks, I had help from Ros with the decorating aspect. Grandad and I handled the layout and building out of the space."

Maddie walked over and placed her bag next to mine. She begins unpacking the items in the bags.

"Wow! That's impressive that y'all did all of this by yourselves. It's so nice, and I'm sure being so close to work makes it even nicer," she says.

"The proximity to work definitely has its benefits," I agree. "What do you need me to do?" I ask once we have everything laid out before us.

"You pick a couple of movies for us to watch while I prep and start the meatballs and sauce. I want to have these in the oven for at least three hours if not four. That is my minimum requirement, so I know the sauce has absorbed all the slow-cooked flavors."

"Hey, now you're sounding like a real chef."

With amusement, she says, "I wouldn't say that, but this dish is something I'm pretty confident cooking."

"Well, I'll leave you to it and go search for a movie or two to watch," I tell her, leaning over and kissing her cheek. Maddie leans into the kiss and sighs. I allow my lips to linger for a second longer than needed.

Maddie busies herself in the kitchen, and I plop myself on the couch. Picking up the remote, I switch on the television and begin scrolling through all the streaming services.

"Comedy? Action? Romance? Or better yet, horror?" I yell over my shoulder to her.

I can hear her moving around the small kitchen behind me.

"Honestly, I love it all. I chose dinner, so you choose the movie."

"Fine, I may just pick one of each, and we'll be up all night."

"Ha! Once the sun goes down, so do my eyelids if I'm

125

watching a movie."

I laugh. "Now you're just sounding like an old woman."

"Just being honest. I can't help it that my eyes have a mind of their own when I feel too relaxed."

"By the way, Gran and Grandad told me something interesting, and I feel a little ashamed I forgot."

"Oh really, this does sound intriguing," she says.

"We've met before," I tell her.

I hear something click against the counter, and her footsteps hurry against the hardwood floors until she stands before me.

"Excuse me?"

I look up at her adorably confused face and say, "Yep."

"No," she says.

"Yep, thirteen years ago when you were here with your grandparents," I tell her, tipping my head to see around her, still scrolling through our movie options. "Gran even gave me proof."

"Huh, well...now I feel like I need to think a little harder," she says, closing her eyes as if that's helping her concentrate.

I laugh at her expression. "Grandad said we were, in his words, 'taken with one another.' But maybe it was one-sided if you don't remember."

Her eyes snap open. "I remember. Oh my God, I remember now."

"But do you remember being taken with me?"

She rolls her eyes, "I remember a boy. I remember we only spent one day together, and the next day, he left while my grandparents and I explored a bit. That was you?"

Tossing the remote onto the couch, I stand up and go over to the bag I had all our picnic stuff in. I had placed the envelope Gran gave me that held the picture of me and little Maddie. Reaching in, I pull out the envelope and walk back to Maddie while she silently watches me. When I'm standing back in front of her, I stick the envelope out for her to take.

"Ya know, I feel like you're avoiding my question," I tease as I plop myself back down on the couch and start searching again.

Maddie laughs and shakes her head as she opens the envelope and pulls out the photo. I watch her from the corner of my eyes as she studies it. Her lips began to curl up at the corners, and I knew she remembered because I had the same reaction when I first saw it.

Looking over at me, she says, "Nah, I don't think I remember you at all."

I can hear the grin in her voice that she's trying to keep from showing. Reaching my arms out and grabbing Maddie around the waist, I pull her on top of me as we both fall on top of the couch. "You lie! I saw it on your face!" I exclaim as she giggles and squirms in my arms like she's trying to get away, but I hold her tight. "You remembered just how smitten you were with me. And to think that was after only knowing me for one day." We both laughed.

"I guess our emotions can't be denied when it comes to one another," she says, amusement in her voice.

Our eyes meet, and suddenly, things don't seem so funny anymore. I'm consumed by an overwhelming desire to have my mouth on hers. From the look in her eyes, Maddie is feeling it too.

I'm not sure which one of us moves first, but our mouths collide, and I'm slipping my tongue between her lips. She moans the moment our tongues begin to tangle together. It's fast and frenzied; then it turns slow and soothing. I sit up a little with her still straddling me. Her hands roam down my back and up under my shirt. I pull her closer to me, and our bodies press together.

Our mouths come apart, both of us panting. "Maddie, I want you so bad," I confess.

"I want you, too." I can see her desire staring back at me, and I'm confident she can feel mine.

She pushes the hair back from her face as she looks down into my eyes. "Are you sure about this because this will mean something to me?" I ask her, keeping our gazes locked.

"I'm certain."

That is all I need to hear; I kiss her once more, but only briefly. "Come on," I say. I lift her off me, and we both stand. Hand in hand, I lead Maddie over to my bed. When we reach the end of the bed, I gently turn her to face me. I want to savor this moment and go slow.

I reach out slowly and caress the side of her face; she closes her eyes and leans in. Turning her head a little, she places a light kiss against the palm of my hand. Maddie opened her eyes and watched me as she deliberately began to unbutton my flannel. I want to touch her, but I hold back to allow her to take a little control.

Once she has my shirt completely unbuttoned, she

pushes it off my shoulder. Then she moves to lift my undershirt up over my head, and I help make that easier until I'm shirtless. I close my eyes as her hands glide over my chest, sending a shiver over my body. Maddie pauses her movement so my lids open, and I find her just staring at me, both of her hands resting palms down on my chest.

Tenderly, I push the cardigan from her shoulders and lift up her camisole. She raises her arms, and I slide the thin silk material over her head.

"You're beautiful," I tell her.

"So are you."

Wrapping my arm around her waist, I pull her to me, taking her mouth with mine once again. When I deepen the kiss, Maddie lets out another of her little soft moans like she did earlier, which makes me want more.

Without breaking our kiss, I move my hands to the waist of her jeans and begin to unbutton them. She follows my lead and unbuttons mine. We push each other's jeans and underwear down. It is only now that we break our kiss and step out of our bottoms. We take one long, slow look at each other's bodies before quickly coming back together. I don't think I could ever get enough of kissing her.

"I love touching you," she says between kisses. Maddie runs her hands over and around my shoulders, down my back, and then back up until she is back to my chest, where she started. "Your body just feels so good under my hands." She keeps touching my body, and all I can think about is how it makes the desire spread to every spot her hands move over. I reach behind her, unhooking her bra and letting it fall to the floor.

My mouth moves to her neck, and I kiss my way down until I reach the curve of her breast. Her head falls back, and her chest pushes toward me like she is begging for more. There's that little moan again, but this time, it's almost a groan.

"Well, I guess we're even because I love kissing you. I want my mouth on every inch of you." My yearning to follow through on my words is apparent in my voice.

"I'm yours to have, Ryder."

Those words create something almost feral-like within me. "Good, because I was planning on staking claim."

Maddie's eyes darken; she reaches up and runs her hands through my hair, gently tightening her grip and pulling my mouth to hers. Our tongues are doing things to one another I've never experienced before. Our kisses were quick, but now the tempo has changed. We take it deeper. Slower.

I push her back with care, and she falls against the bed. I fall with her, making sure I don't put all my weight on her. I begin kissing her from her mouth, across her cheek, and over to her shoulder. I keep this path on her body until I reach her left breast and her perky little nipple. Taking it in between my lips, I suckle on it, eliciting a quiet whimper from her lips. Her hand is back in my hair, slightly pulling me down. It feels so good. I want to be in her now.

"Ryder, I want you in me, please," she begs when I move to the other breast.

"Not yet."

Another whimper escapes her as my tongue circles the sensitive area of her breast. Giving her pleasure feels so satisfying and better than I could've imagined. I continue moving my lips and tongue down over her flat belly to each inner thigh. Pressing her legs open lightly with my hand, I start to move to her center but stop and lift my head to look up at her. Her eyes are closed, and her facial expression shows pure pleasure. I lower my head briefly and swipe her center with my tongue. She gasps, "Ryder!"

"Does that feel good, baby?"

I don't give her a chance to answer; I lean in again and put my whole mouth over her, sucking her clitoris. She cries out again, and her hands are back in my hair. The more I suck, the tighter her hold becomes. One second, she's pulling me closer, and the next, she's pushing me back. I can feel her pulsating in my mouth; then, suddenly, she's crying out my name. I don't stop until she is silent again. I can hear her labored breathing when I raise my head and kiss my way back up to her mouth. I look down at her face. Her eyes are closed, but then they open, and a smile slowly spreads across her face.

"I need you inside me now, please."

I kiss her lips quickly. "And I need to be inside of you." I roll to my side and reach out, opening the drawer of my bedside table to grab some protection. Once I'm ready, I roll back over until I'm hovering above her again. When our gazes lock, I slowly move my hips forward until just the tip of me has entered her. Her eyes darken again, growing more expansive, and so does her smile. This time, I'm the one groaning in pleasure.

Maddie wrapped her arms around me and rubbed her hands down my back.

"I can't wait any longer," I say between gritted teeth.

"Then don't."

We moan in pleasure together. Soon, her hips are rolling into me, and mine are thrusting into her.

There is something about being inside Maddie that's different. Perfect. Fulfilling. Emotional. She feels so damn good, and this feels better than I've ever felt before. Suddenly, I feel her tightening around me, and that same familiar feeling courses through me until we both fall over the edge. Both of us gasping one another's name until we've met our release and can't move anymore.

Maddie pulls me to her chest, and I go willingly, exhausted from the exertion of making love.

I roll to face her and kiss the side of her head. She looks at me, and a sweet, satisfied smile covers her face. She places a kiss on my lips, then rests her head on my shoulder and closes her eyes.

I allow myself to watch her as she drifts off to sleep. Soon, my own eyes begin to feel heavy from exhaustion and close too.

CHAPTER 20

Maddie

When the chime of the oven sounds to indicate the pre-heat cycle is finished, I cringe a little. Glancing quickly in the direction of Ryder's bed, where he is still sleeping, I look to see if the oven has woken him. But he's still in the same position he was when I slipped out of bed twenty minutes ago.

I quietly slide the pot full of sauce and meatballs into the oven to cook and gently close the door. I set a timer on my watch and started to clean up the mess. I'm only slightly disappointed the meatballs will only be able to cook for a couple of hours now since we fell asleep after... well, after.

When I'd thought about making love to Ryder, I always feared I would feel awkward, but it was the complete opposite. I'm happy and at ease with everything that has happened between us. I rinse off the last dish I used while prepping and turn to find a set of pale green eyes looking at me from across the room.

"Hey," Ryder says, his voice still a little sleepy, which sounds sexy as hell. His head is propped up on his hand while he lies on his side on the bed, his hair messy and his smile crooked.

"Hey," I say back as I dry my hands off and start to walk toward him.

When I reach the edge of the bed, Ryder moves quickly and pulls me down to him before I know what is happening. I laugh as he cradles me in his arms. He looks deep into my eyes, and I can see he wants to kiss me. And he does—his lips gently caress mine. It seems like I can't control myself when he kisses me because I always seem to moan from pure satisfaction. Nothing has ever felt as good as his lips on mine.

When he stopped kissing me, I grinned up at him, and then I whispered, "We have at least two hours before the food is done."

Without hesitation, his lips are back on mine, and before long, they're touching every inch of my naked body.

Right now, I'm not so sure I could ever get enough of Ryder Evans, his soft lips, his expressive eyes, or the way his body moves against mine.

• • •

A few hours later, Ryder and I are sitting on each end of his couch facing one another with big bowls of pasta and meatballs in our hands.

"This is quite literally the best sauce and meatballs I

have ever tasted," he says between bites. His eyes close in contentment, and he groans a little. I can't help feeling a little pride in myself.

"Thanks."

"Seriously, don't tell Gran I said that because I wouldn't want to hurt her feelings," he says, laughing.

"I wouldn't dare," I laugh.

"Where did you learn to make this? Is it an old family recipe?"

"Yes. It's been passed down my mama's side of the family. It's something we cook together and put a lot of love into," I tell him. "But honestly, I didn't really make it the right way tonight. I was a bit preoccupied." I actually blush when I say this.

"Well, you must have remembered to add the love part because it tastes perfect to me. If it can get better than this, then I would say you need to open a restaurant."

"Ryder, I'm not sure a person would find much success opening a restaurant with one menu item. No matter how good it tastes." My lips lift at the corners in amusement.

He smiles with his mouth full and says, "Ya never know."

Shaking my head, I take another bite. Between bites, I say, "Tell me about your life, your childhood...tell me everything."

He gets a sort of far-off look for a minute, and I worry I've asked too much. But then he seems to come back to the present.

"Well, Rosalind and I had fun and loving parents. They were always very affectionate to us and to each other. Our mom's parents passed away a really long time ago, so we never knew them. We had Gran and Grandad, who are my dad's parents. We visited often from Santa Barbara, where we lived back then." He pauses, taking a bite of his food.

I consider saying something, but it feels like he isn't done and actually wants to keep talking. So, I remain silent, eating my food.

"My parents were pretty incredible. I mean, Jonathan and Jessica, as perfectly as their names go together, so did their love for one another. One weekend, when I was thirteen, Rosalind and I were visiting Gran and Grandad, and then that weekend turned into forever. My parents were gone, and our world turned upside down. I don't know who took it harder, me and Ros or my grandparents. My dad was their only kid, and they had a close relationship."

I put my bowl down and reached out, allowing my hand to rest on Ryder's knee. He gives me a half smile. "Ryder, I can't imagine that kind of pain. The pain you must have felt. Thirteen is too young to lose your parents."

"Yeah, it took a while for it to feel real. For life to start feeling normal again."

"I'm so sorry for your pain."

"That's one thing that never changes, the painful feeling of that loss. It's morphed so life can move forward, but when I think of them, the life they've missed, the hugs I never got to have, and the words of encouragement left unsaid, it's just as painful as the day it happened."

I have no words, so I don't respond.

"But life here has been everything we could have hoped for. Ros and I are lucky because our grandparents are kind, loving, and good. We had an amazing childhood, and I know it was everything our parents would've wanted for us had they been here to give it to us themselves."

"I'm glad you had them."

When he looks at me, his smile is wider than a moment ago. "Enough about all of that; tell me more about you."

"Like, what?"

"Like, everything."

"Okay…well, umm, I grew up in the same small town my entire life. We had one stop light. I went to school with the same kids from preschool through high school. I have an older brother and sister. My parents are still married after forty-one years and are as happy as ever. Like you, they are fun and loving and so in love."

"I love that," he says with a grin.

"Me, too. I'm the baby of the family, but I'm the 'doer,' the one everyone leans on in a way. My family is everything to me."

I told him more about my childhood and the town I grew up in. I talk my family, college, and Connor.

It feels good and easy to share things with him. Ryder is a good listener—quiet and only commenting when appropriate. Our conversation almost felt therapeutic because while I lived it, I'd never talked about how I felt about anything in my life this way.

"Do you miss him?" Ryder suddenly asks.

"Who?"

"Connor. Do you miss him? I mean, you were together longer than a lot of marriages last. I'm just wondering if you miss him at all…wish things were different."

I think about what he's asking me. When I answer, I want to make sure I'm clear because I want him to really understand how I feel.

"You're right. Connor and I were together for a long time. I love him and never thought about loving anyone else. That was before he did what he did and said the things he said. I was devastated when he cheated and hurt me for a long time. It hurts some even now, but I haven't thought about him since I arrived. Connor wanted a different life, which is what we're living—different lives. I'm happier than I could've ever imagined," I explain, never breaking eye contact with Ryder, hoping he understands what I'm trying to say.

He waits for a beat, then says, "I'm happy you're happy. I'm happy, too."

Ryder stands, picks up our bowls from the coffee table, and walks over to the sink. I stand up and follow behind him.

"You cooked; therefore, I clean," he says.

"Okay, I like this deal," I respond, smiling.

I lean against the kitchen island while he washes the dishes and puts the leftovers in containers.

"I will probably bring this to Billy tomorrow. I usually bring him my leftovers."

"That's nice of you. Does Billy work for you?"

"Yeah, he's just a kid trying to make something of himself. Sam and I hired him a little while ago. We've taken him under our wing and try to help him out any way we can," he explains.

"That's sweet."

"I don't know about sweet. I was nineteen once, and lucky I had Gran to feed me. Billy is a little way from home, so not much a nineteen-year-old boy can cook when he's renting a room in a house share, you know?" Ryder wipes his hands dry and turns to face me. He leans back and doesn't say anything as he stares at me.

I nervously glance at my watch and see it's almost eight-thirty. "I guess it's getting kind of late; maybe I should head home."

Ryder pushes off the counter and walks over to me. "Maddie, stay with me."

"Stay?" I question.

"Yes, stay the night with me," he says before continuing, "I mean, if you want to."

"Do you want me to stay?"

He smiles, "Yes, that's why I asked. Stay."

For a moment, I think of every reason I shouldn't, but none seem like a real reason to say no when everything in me wants to say yes. "Yes."

"Yes, you'll stay?"

"Yes."

Ryder's grin grows wider. "Yes. I like that answer a lot. It will make sleep a lot sweeter because it has been close to a month and a half since I've had a good, restful night's sleep."

"Hey, I got here a month and a half ago."

"I know, and you've been on my mind every night since."

Ryder takes my hand and pulls me to him. He's going to kiss me again, and I'm absolutely here for it. As soon as the thought crosses my mind, his lips are on mine. Slow and soft, allowing me to feel everything he feels for me. I kiss him back with the same gentleness.

Saying yes to staying the night with Ryder tonight was just an opening to a doorway, and this kiss is the key to what is possible on the other side.

CHAPTER 21

Ryder

I wasn't joking when I told Maddie last night that her staying with me would allow me to get my first peaceful night's sleep since she arrived. When I wake up this morning, I realize I've slept in later than usual for the first time in as long as I can remember. Plus, it was really good sleep. It probably helped that I was up later than usual and quite a bit more physical than expected.

I can't help the grin tickling at the corner of my lips with that thought.

Maddie is still sleeping soundly next to me. I'm lying on my side, watching her. Her breathing is soft. She looks calm and at peace. Her creamy skin is nearly perfect, and I get the urge to touch it, so I do as tenderly as possible. She barely stirs beneath my touch.

What am I doing here? How did we get to this point so quickly? To the point where I can barely remember life before her. Yesterday, we discussed how fast all of this was moving. But we also agreed we would embrace it and allow it to unfold as we went because we wanted to ensure we got what this might be just because it seemed like it was going too fast. Now, it matters even less how fast things are moving. All that matters now is that I want Maddie in my life; apparently, she wants me in hers.

"Mornin."

Her voice is low and sleepy but pulls me from my thoughts. A touch of her Southern accent adds to the already sweet-sounding greeting. She's slightly covering her mouth, but I can see the smile on her lips from behind her hand.

"Good morning, gorgeous," I say, leaning forward and placing a quick peck on her forehead.

Groggily, she asks, "What time is it?"

Unsure of the time because, honestly, I was too busy watching her, I rolled to my back and looked over at the clock hanging in the kitchen. Whoa, it's nine o'clock in the morning. I really did sleep in late. I knew by the light coming through the windows it was later than usual, but I didn't think it was quite this late. I roll back to my side and face her again. "It's nine."

She yawns like she hasn't just woken up and says through the yawn, "Wow, I think I was fifteen the last time I slept until nine o'clock in the morning. It's nice that Evelyn gave me the weekend off." Her stomach gives a little grumble.

"Hungry?" I smile.

"Starving," she replies. "Coffee sounds even better. Maybe coffee than food?"

"Perfect, my thoughts exactly." I roll over and out of bed. I grab my discarded t-shirt from the floor and make my way into the kitchen. "You stay right where you're at, and I'll start the coffee."

"You don't have to tell me twice."

When I glance over my shoulder, Maddie buries herself deeper in the comforter. I smile.

"You know, I realize I don't have any breakfast food. I'm kind of a run across to Dream Bean Cafe in the morning kind of guy."

I hear a giggle from the bed. "Well, that's fine. You won't have to twist my arm to talk me into one of their pastries."

"Good, we'll have one cup of coffee while we throw on some clothes, then head over."

I place a K-cup into the Keurig, then place a cup underneath the spout. "Cream?"

"Please, and thank you."

"Sugar?"

"Nope."

Maddie's coffee finishes brewing, and I put it aside and then start a cup for myself. Once I have both cups made, I carry them over to the bed. She peeks out from beneath the blankets and pushes herself into a sitting position.

"Here ya go," I say, handing Maddie her cup of coffee.

She eagerly takes it from my hands and begins to cool it by blowing on it. "Thank you." When she takes her first sip, Maddie moans in appreciation.

"Good, huh?"

"Better than good. Amazing."

I move around to the opposite side of the bed and climb next to her. We both sit in silence for a moment, enjoying our coffee.

Maddie is the first to break the silence. "So, have you always wanted to be a mechanic? I know you went to college, but it wasn't mechanic school, right?"

"Yes and no. I've always wanted to be a mechanic, but my grandparents wanted us to make sure we had an education to fall back on. So, I majored in business and then came home and started working in the mechanic shop for Eddie until he was ready to sell it. My best friend Sam and I decided to go into business together, and here we are, mechanic shop owners."

"What about you? Have you always wanted to work in an inn?"

She grins, "I wouldn't say an inn or bed and breakfast exactly. But I have always wanted to go into the hospitality industry one day in some capacity. Whether it was owning my own bed and breakfast or just working at a nice hotel that adds all the little special touches that make a destination unique." Her lips tip up in a sort of sad smile. "I never would have moved here if my grandparents hadn't suggested it. Now, I can't imagine being anywhere else, even though I miss my family and Texas more than I can explain."

"I'm sorry you had to leave your family, but I can't say I'm sorry you're here."

Maddie looks over at me, and we hold one another's gazes for a split second.

"I'm not sorry either."

"Good."

"But I am sorry we have to leave this bed right now because I'm starving, and if I don't get some food in me soon, you will meet hangry Maddie, and that is not an attractive look on me at all." She sets her cup on the bedside table and throws the comforter off her lap. Hopping out of bed, she searches around the room for her clothes, wearing nothing but her skimpy little panties and one of my t-shirts.

"If you don't find your clothes soon, we aren't going anywhere but right back into this bed," I laugh.

She gives me a wink over her shoulder and then turns, holding her jeans in the air. "My stomach wins."

"Damn, woman. You're a tease."

Laughing, I get up and begin getting dressed myself. Much to Maddie's relief, I have an extra toothbrush, and once we're ready, we're on our way.

Just before we walk out of my apartment, I pull her to me and kiss her long and hard. We reluctantly end the kiss, and she looks at me and says, "I almost said we should skip breakfast, then you pulled away from our kiss."

"I can easily pick up where I left off."

"Nope, too late," she giggles, then backs away and out the door.

"Cruel...so cruel," I say as I lock the door behind us.

• • •

As we walked through the door of Dream Bean Cafe, I spotted Molly behind the counter.

"Ryder! Maddie! You're here. Together again."

Maddie and I look at each other and laugh. It's pretty cute how Molly seems to be interested in our relationship.

"Yes, we are," I say as I look in her direction. "And we would both like a cup of coffee."

"And a couple of cheese and cherry pastries," Maddie adds.

Molly grins from ear to ear. "No problem. So, what are you two up to this very early Saturday morning?"

"We are up to breakfast and just being together," Maddie replies nonchalantly.

She says as Molly passes us the pastries and coffee over the counter. "That sounds VERY…nice."

Maddie and I grab our drinks and breakfast, and while I pay, Maddie keeps the teasing tone going with Molly. "It is VERRRRRYYYY nice to be with Ryder."

Molly's cheeks turn red, and her smile is so big it looks like it might hurt.

"Bye, Molly." Maddie and I say in unison as we walk toward the door.

"Maddie, in case you're wondering, I totally approve," Molly calls out just before we leave the shop.

We pause momentarily, look at one another again, and laugh out loud. It's a beautiful day, and since the bed and breakfast is only a three- to five-minute walk from my apartment, we decided to take advantage.

We walk a few feet down the sidewalk, walking toward the bed and breakfast, before Maddie says, "Molly is the sweetest, most precocious, and nosiest fourteen-year-old I've ever met, and honestly, that is saying something."

"She's something alright. Honestly, she's been that

way since she could talk." And we both find ourselves laughing again.

Walking side by side through town, I listen to her talk about everything she loves about this little town I've spent most of my life in. I find myself seeing it from a new perspective. I've always loved it, but the way Maddie sees Cambria gives it a sort of magical semblance about it.

Before I knew it, we were walking up the driveway of the bed and breakfast toward her cottage in the back.

"You know Gran will expect both of us at Sunday dinner tonight, right?"

"I've come to learn that her invitations to Sunday dinner aren't optional but a requirement," she says as we round one of the big trees lining the driveway. "And honestly, I'm okay with it. The food is delicious, and the company is nice, too."

"I've always loved the tradition of Sunday night dinner, set aside for us to stay connected, but since you've been here, they've taken on a whole new meaning."

She angles her body toward me as she walks and says, "I'm taking that as a compliment." Then she turns back, taking a sip from her drink.

"Good, because that's how I meant for you to take it."

With my empty hand, I take hold of hers and intertwine our fingers together. Maddie squeezes my hand lightly once our palms come together.

As we approached her front porch, I laughed.

"What?"

"Nothing really; I just remembered how mad you were that first morning we met. You came blazing out of that front door, off the porch, and around the car so fast with barely a thing covering your body."

She laughs, "Not true, I had pajamas on."

"If that's what you call those tiny little shorts."

"It is what I call them and also what Victoria's Secret calls them for your information."

We step onto the porch, and I lift my hands in mock defense. "Fine. Fine. You were so hot, that's all, and it took me by surprise."

"You're the one who took me by surprise."

"Well, you got under my skin from the very second you yelled at me," I tell her. Then, just before she opened her front door, I snaked my arm around her waist and pulled her to me. "And now, you're all I think about."

Her lips tip up at the corners, and she says, "Well, that makes two of us."

It's been at least an hour since we last kissed, and I'm not about to wait a minute longer. My mouth took hers, and she willingly opened hers to mine. It is sweet and sexy and unfortunately short because I suddenly remember that we undoubtedly have an audience peering at us from the front house. When I end the kiss, I gently peck her nose before pulling away. Maddie's lips look well-kissed and pouty.

"Don't give me that look. I realize this may not be as private of a moment as it might seem," I say, tipping my head toward the front house.

She glances in that direction, and her mouth forms an oh.

"Do you wanna come in?"

"I think I'm gonna run up to the front and talk to my grandparents, then go home, change, and clean up before dinner."

"Stay with me after dinner," she blurts out.

"Really?"

"Yeah, I...is it too much...too quick? I know we talked about how quickly this is all going, but if you ..."

I place my finger gently over her lips. "Shhh, it's not too much. I was making sure. Yes, I will bring a little bag because I have to work in the morning. "

"Do you think Evelyn and Henry will be upset with us?"

"Nah, I think they're already thinking way past over-nighters in our relationship at this point," I tease while trying to reassure her, too.

She slightly shakes her head at my comment, then leans forward and places one last soft kiss on my lips.

"See you in a bit," she says as she opens her door.

Whew, those lips on mine mess with my head.

"Yeah, see you soon."

Maddie closes the door, and I walk up to the main house, mentally preparing myself for more questions. I don't mind, though, because nothing can shake these feelings I'm having for Maddie.

CHAPTER 22

Maddie

When I shut the door behind me, I fall against it and close my eyes. I feel giddy with so many happy emotions; I can barely contain them any longer. The weeks have rolled by as I have fallen into my new routine: Get up early, work hard, do afternoon errands, and evenings either on the phone with Ryder or exploring my new town with him. Then these last twenty-four hours have been even more incredible, overwhelming, and full of so many unexpected emotions.

Pushing away from the door, I go down the hall to my bedroom. I grab a change of clothes and a towel and head into the bathroom. Turning the shower nozzle on, I undress while I wait for the water to get hot. My muscles are a little tired and sore. The thought brings a slow smile to my face.

While I wash my hair, my mind drifts to the way Ryder touched me and the way it felt to have him inside me.

Having never been with someone else in such an intimate way besides Connor, I didn't know it could feel so different. I never knew I could be the most essential part of our lovemaking. Ryder made me feel as if my pleasure was his priority and then made us become one until we both felt complete satisfaction. And it wasn't just the first time, but every time we did it until we both couldn't move and finally fell asleep.

Stepping out of the shower, I dry myself and put on fresh, clean clothes.

Then I realized that if Ryder is staying over tonight, I need to change my sheets and straighten up a bit. I tackle these few chores and then look at my watch. It's been a couple of hours since he left, and there's still at least three more hours until dinner.

I grab a book and my phone before heading to the porch and sit in one of the rockers. It's another perfect day, sunny with a slight breeze. Luckily, the front house and all of the trees in the yard help block the wind a bit.

I curl my feet under me and lean back, closing my eyes for a few minutes.

Suddenly, my phone vibrates, alerting me that a call is coming in. Caro's face fills the screen. I quickly swipe to answer it.

"Seriously, how do you do it?" I ask as I answer the phone.

"Hello to you, too. And how do I do what?" she responds.

"Call me when I'm wrestling with things that make me anxious and unsure what to do."

"Huh, well, I would like to say it's because I'm psychic, but I honestly think I'm just so nosey that when too much time goes in between us talking, I think there must be things you aren't sharing with me. So, I call to get the scoop and live vicariously through you."

Shaking my head, I laugh.

"You're so weird."

"As I tell the kids, name-calling isn't very kind."

I laugh again.

"Yeah...yeah. How are you? Everything okay?"

"I'm great; it's life as usual over here. And every day here is basically Groundhog Day," she says. "What about you? What's got you so anxious and contemplative?"

"Contemplative?" I ask, laughing again. "That is one way to describe what I'm doing."

"Spill it."

"Oh, Caro, I followed your advice when I had only been here a few weeks."

"Awesome!" she exclaims through the phone before continuing, "And what advice was that?"

"Your advice about letting myself loose and feeling what I feel."

"Aha! Yes, and do the grandson."

"What the hell, Caro?"

"Okay, maybe that isn't exactly what I said, but it was definitely what I was thinking."

"You're really too much sometimes," I tell her.

"Thank you." I can hear her smile through the phone. "Now seriously, what's on your mind, Sis."

I clear my throat and let the silence hang between us for a moment. One thing about Caroline is she may be sarcastic and silly, but she is also a great listener, patient, and wise.

"Well, I started seeing Ryder. We went on a date recently, and it was after a heavy make-out session."

"Thank you, Jesus!"

"Caro, there is something about him. We click, and it's like we both took our shoes off and jumped feet first into this whole thing." I pause again, then quickly say, "We slept together, and I stayed over at his place."

"Madelyn Marie Jennings! You floozy!" Caroline blurts through the phone.

Covering my phone with my free hand, I say, "Oh my God, I know! Mama and Daddy would be so disappointed!"

Caroline begins to laugh uncontrollably through the phone.

"Stop laughing!"

"Geez, Maddie! I was kidding. You're twenty-six years old. You just slept with the second guy you've ever shown interest in. As for Mama and Daddy, they would have preferred we both waited until marriage, but that isn't the reality these days. So, stop and tell me what's really bothering you. Was he bad in bed?"

"My gosh, no! Caro, I told you we clicked, and the sex was…was incredible. Like I never imagined, it seemed to get better each time."

"Oh, okay…each time," she says.

I giggle.

"Still not hearing a problem here, Madds."

"The problem or…not problem is that I've known him

a month and there are feelings. Big feelings. And it's a little scary."

"Maddie, time…when it's right, time doesn't matter. What matters is that you're happy, and he's happy and that you're both on the same page."

"I think we are because we sort of talked about it."

"So then, I don't see the problem."

I sigh, "I don't know. Maybe I'm just thinking that if my heart didn't have it right with Connor after twelve years, how could it get it right after one month."

"You're overthinking this, Madds. Not to mention, that was young love. Give yourself a break, and just let your heart do the decision-making. Your head is what gets you in trouble when it comes to love."

"I think that might be the most backward advice you've ever given me, but I like it."

"Backward as it may be to you when our heart and gut are trying to say something, we often dismiss them because we're told our brain is where the intelligence is."

"I said, fine! You're right, and I will stop overthinking it and go with what my heart and gut are telling me," I tell her.

"In my life, there have never been sweeter words spoken by any person than 'You're right.'"

"You're also ridiculous, but that is all a part of your charm."

Caroline laughs, and I realize how good it feels to talk this out with her. I spend way too much time overthinking life, and well if I would just quit holding these things in, I would probably have a lot less anxiety.

"I love you, Madds. I better get going. Call Mama and Daddy so they stop asking me if I've talked to you this week," Caroline says.

"I love you, too. And I will as soon as we hang up. Give the monkeys and Rob big hugs and love from me."

"Good, and you got it. I'm sure they send theirs back to you."

I hang up with my sister and feel so much more at ease. As promised, I dialed my parent's number and waited for them to answer. I look forward to hearing their voices because a week is too long.

"Hey, Mama."

"Hey, baby girl."

And those three simple words are all I need to make this day even better.

• • •

After talking to my parents, I spent the rest of the afternoon reading on my little porch. I even dozed off for a short nap, which rejuvenated me after the long night.

Now, I spray myself with a perfume that leaves a light floral scent lingering in the air. There's a soft knock on my front door, so I give myself one final look in the hallway mirror as I pass it on the way to let Ryder in.

A smile spreads across my face as I open the door and see Ryder. "Hi," I say.

"Hey, beautiful."

It has barely been five hours since I saw him, but I feel an overwhelming sense of happiness when I see him. He's casual and sexy without even trying, which is more appealing than I ever thought possible.

He leans in and places his lips on mine for a brief kiss. Pulling back, he says, "You ready to walk up to the front house?"

"I'm ready."

Reaching down, he takes my hand into his, and we close the door behind us. As we walk across the lawn, the sun is only barely shining in the evening sky. Dusk has settled over the bed and breakfast, and there's a soft glow coming from each window of the occupied rooms and the kitchen, where I'm sure Evelyn is moving about, getting things ready for dinner.

"It's a nice night out," I say as we walk hand in hand.

"It is. The day was pretty, too. What did you do with your free afternoon?"

"I talked to my sister and my parents. Then, I read and took a little nap on the front porch. It felt perfect. What about you?"

"Sounds like an amazing way to spend your afternoon. I visited with my grandparents a little before I went home. Then, I just cleaned up myself and my apartment. I packed a bag for the night and even took a little nap myself."

"I think I needed it because I definitely didn't get much sleep last night," I say with a coy smile.

Ryder chuckles, "Yeah, I know what you mean."

The back door swings open as we approach, and Ros is standing there, hands on her hips and a grin on her face. "I heard Grandad telling Gran that Maddie didn't come home last night."

Shaking his head, Ryder says, "Good lord, Rosalind. Mind your business much?"

I can't help the giggle that escapes. Ryder looks over at me. "Don't encourage her, Maddie. She has no boundaries or couth."

"Oh, give me a break," Ros retorts as she rolls her eyes.

I laugh again, "Well, I have siblings, and there is no such thing as privacy or mindin' your own business in the household I grew up in."

Rosa steps back inside the house, and we follow behind her.

"Thanks, Maddie."

"No problem, but Ryder is right. It's none of your business if I came home or not."

It's Ryder's turn to start laughing, and Ros throws us both a feigning look of hurt from my loose support of Ryder.

When the three of us walk into the eat-in kitchen, Henry is setting the table, and Evelyn is pulling something that smells incredible from the oven.

"Good evening, you two. Nice of you to join us," Henry says.

"I hope you all brought your appetites because I made enough food to feed a small army," Evelyn announces.

"I'm starving," Henry says.

Evelyn swats him gently on his arm, "I wasn't talking to you, Mister."

"How was I supposed to know?"

"Well, I'm starving too, if it makes you feel any better, Evelyn," I say as I walk over to give them both a hug.

As she welcomed my embrace, Evelyn said, "I was hoping you would be."

"Me, too, Gran," Ryder and Ros say in unison, then look at one another and roll their eyes.

I love their sibling interactions. It makes me miss Caroline and Jake more than I thought possible.

"Good, let's all sit down. Grandad already has the table all set, and I'll bring over the pot roast."

We take a seat, and Ryder sits in the chair next to mine. Ros sits across from me, and Evelyn and Henry take each end of the table. Henry leads us in a short prayer before we all dig in. We all chat about what a lovely day it was and what we did with our time this afternoon. Everyone had a full day, and we were glad to be together and eat a good meal.

So much about these dinners reminds me of the years we spent going to my grandparents' house. I love how vital Sunday dinners are to Evan's family because it was the same for me when I was growing up. It's also nice to have a little piece of tradition from home here.

"Do you have a lot of work this coming week, Ryder?" Henry asks before he spoons a mouthful of mashed potatoes into his mouth.

"Work is pretty steady, which is good, and walk-in customers fill in where we don't have appointments set. We've been fortunate," Ryder explains.

"That's great, Ry," Evelyn praises. "We have a little bit of a down week until next Sunday—only about one check-in every couple of days this week. But next Sunday, we'll have five check-outs and check-ins, so our turnaround will keep me and Maddie busy. Speaking of, Rosalind, we will definitely need you for as much time as you can spare that day. I know you said you will need time to prepare for finals, so whatever you can do will be appreciated."

"I'm actually excited about the prospect of a full day. It will make things fun and allow us to try out some of the new ideas we've been tossing around," I chime in.

"I'll be able to make time. I agree, Maddie; I'm looking forward to using that new check-in software we found," Rosalind says.

The conversation continues to flow during dinner and even into dessert. And no one brought up mine and Ryder's new relationship. There wasn't any awkwardness. Once we finished eating, Ryder, Ros, and I volunteered to clean up so Evelyn and Henry could relax.

After we were done cleaning, Rosalind was the first to leave, claiming she had homework.

"So, Maddie, did Ryder show you the photo of the two of you I gave him?" Evelyn asks as she takes a sip of hot tea from her mug.

"He did; it was so sweet. Honestly, I didn't remember meeting him at first, but that photo brought it full circle and made me really think about my visit. Then, it felt like it was only yesterday."

"Yeah, I remember Ryder not wanting to leave to go home, but Jessica and Jonathan made it clear they had to stick to their plans and get you all home. He never said why he wanted to stay so bad, but we knew," Henry says, looking over and waggling his eyebrows at Ryder.

"Seriously, Grandad, maybe I just wanted to stay with

you and Gran," Ryder says.

I laugh, "I do remember I was disappointed."

"It was cute the way you two just sort of hit it off and instantly became smitten," Evelyn adds.

"Well, she was the prettiest girl I had ever seen," Ryder admits. "She changed my whole view on girls that year. Actually, a lot changed that year."

Ryder gets a far-off, sad look in his eyes.

"Yeah, it was only a few months later that we lost your parents."

I reach over and place my hand over Ryder's hand. He looks over in my direction and gives me a crooked, sad smile. My heart hurts for him. I can't imagine losing my parents, especially at that young age.

"Love you, Ryder, my boy. Be sweet to our Maddie. She's a good one," Henry says as he reaches over and pats the top of my hand that's resting over Ryder's hand.

"There's nothing to worry about there, Grandad," Ryder tells him. "Ready?" Ryder asks, looking over at me. "We should let these two get to their usual nightly wind-down routine."

I nod. "Ready."

We both stand, and so do Evelyn and Henry. They come around the table and give each of us a hug. We all say our goodnights as we make our way to the back door.

As we make our way back across the yard to my little cottage, Ryder and I remain silent, once again holding hands. I look around and notice the starry sky above. It's a bit chilly out now, and I shiver from the cold air that blows through the trees surrounding us.

"Let's pick up the pace and get you out of this cold night air."

Squeezing Ryder's hand, I say, "Yes, let's get in the house. Are you sure you want to stay over still?"

We reach the front door, and Ryder opens it for me. "You aren't getting rid of me now. I'm going to go grab my bag that I left in the truck, and I'll be right back."

He starts to turn toward the door but stops short and turns back around until he's facing me again. He snakes his arm around my waist, pulling me to him and kissing me long and hard like it's going to be our last kiss. It's over before I know it, and he's out the door, leaving me standing there in sudden anticipation of the night to come.

CHAPTER 23

Ryder

Even before I open my eyes, I can sense the difference in my surroundings. I'm definitely not in my bed because these sheets are way softer than mine. They also have this calming lavender scent to them. And then I realize these sheets aren't the only thing soft against my skin. Maddie. My thoughts are overtaken with memories of last night.

We spent another night together, where I studied every inch of her body, from the dimple on her left cheek to the tiny scar from a childhood tree-climbing accident to the pale pink hue of her painted toes. Every inch of her is smooth and kissable. And that's precisely what I did.

I stretch my arms above my head and roll onto my side to face my sleeping beauty. Her eyes are still closed, and her breathing is slow and hushed. This is the second morning I've watched Maddie sleeping. It's something so intimate, and I love how much she trusts me to be able to sleep this peacefully with me next to her.

I scoot a little closer and place a light kiss on her shoulder. I glance up at her face, and she's still in the same position. So, I kiss her on her collarbone. This time, she stirred in her sleep a little, and I took her tiny whimper and the way she pushed against me as permission to continue. I move my mouth to her neck, and her head falls to the side for more, so I carry on, placing another kiss just beneath her chin. I don't linger there long, and finally, I land on her mouth. She is ready for me because she opens her mouth to greet mine, and the way we both sink into one another is so perfect.

Maddie's hands wrapped around me and moved up and down my back. She pulls me to her, and I'm now hovering over the top of her. Our mouths never break contact. My hands begin to slide down her sides until I reach the edge of her lacy panties and begin to inch them down.

When we finally come up for air, my name slips from her lips, "Ryder…"

My God, my name has never sounded so good leaving someone's lips. It only encourages me to keep going, and I slide her panties the rest of the way down. She helps by removing them entirely, then comes back up and slips her tongue into my mouth, and we begin the kissing dance all over again.

She pushes softly at my shoulder until I roll over. Maddie ends up on top of me, and she moves my briefs down my legs and off entirely before she straddles me. I reach over to the side table so I can make sure we're protected.

Maddie lifts her tank top over her head and tosses it

aside. She looks down at me and smiles. She is so perfect. The early morning light barely allows me a view of our pert, full breasts. I reach up and take one in my hand, massaging it gently as she lifts herself up and slides down on me until I'm fully inside her.

We both begin to move together, our motions fluid and in sync. We touch and kiss and savor one another until we are both sent over the edge and unable to move any longer. Maddie collapses on my chest. I kiss the top of her head.

She slides down next to me until she's cradled against me, and my arms are wrapped around her. Maddie places a kiss on my hands and pulls my arms tighter around her.

"I could spend every morning with you this exact way," I whisper against her ear.

"Me, too."

I need to be at work in an hour, but I decide to savor this moment with Maddie a little longer. We both lie there in one another's arms without saying a word until we have no choice but to begin our day.

• • •

When I walked into the shop, Sam and Billy had already opened up and begun preparing for the day. I knew they were going to beat me, so I took the liberty of picking up some donuts and coffee for all of us.

"Good morning," I say as I set the donuts down on the breakroom table and then hand each of them a cup of coffee.

"Well, good morning," Sam says, eyeing me a little

suspiciously. "What's got you so chipper this morning?"

"I bet it's that new pretty girl I heard Mrs. Rogers telling Becky she saw Ryder with the other morning, and that was after she saw them having dinner together a while back," Billy tells him, grinning from ear to ear like a cat who just ate a canary.

"Watch it," I say, half serious, half teasing. "She has a name, and maybe it is Maddie who has me smiling a little brighter these days."

Billy puts his hands up in the air and steps away, snatching a donut in the process. Sam laughs but keeps his eyes on me. In usual fashion, he's going to wait for me to say more without prying any further.

First, I look at Billy. "What did I tell you about listening to the town gossip? Don't."

"Sorry, man. Did I let the cat out of the bag?" Billy asks, stuffing the other half of the donut in his mouth.

Sam guffaws again and shakes his head. "Just stop talking, Billy," he says.

Billy takes a sip of his hot coffee without saying another word.

"I'm in a good mood because I'm happy and have no reason not to be." I take my own donut from the box and take a bite. "But, yes, I am seeing the new girl in town. Her name is Madelyn Jennings. She moved here from Texas to work for my grandparents. We've hit it off, and we are just seeing where this thing is taking us. Okay?"

"Ryder, man, that's cool. It's been years since I've seen you interested in anything other than this shop," Sam says.

"Yeah, man, I know. There's just something about her."

"Like she's hot?" Billy blurts out.

"That's not what I'm talking about at all," I say, wishing Billy was standing a little closer so I could smack him on the back of his head for that comment. He's not, so I continue, "There is something different about her. When I'm with her, I feel like I can be who and what I am without apology."

"But why specifically her?" Billy asks.

"I can't put my finger on a specific thing. It's just a feeling. I want to be with her. Help her. Protect her. Make her laugh."

"Whoa there, buddy! This sounds serious. And the fact that you stayed overnight at her place is out of character for you," Sam chimes in.

"She stayed at my house the night before," I state so plainly, although I know this is going to throw Sam for a loop even more.

"Ryder…man, you're sure about this?" Sam says.

"Yeah, I am. I mean, it feels like I am. The thing is, Sam, I've tried not to overthink things and go with what feels right."

"Okay, you sound sure, so I will have to believe you," Sam states.

"Being with Maddie feels right," I confirm.

Sam stands up from his chair and walks over to me. His facial expression is thoughtful as he places a hand on my shoulder. "I'm happy for you. Just be careful. Are you two on the same page? Have you told her how you're feeling?" Sam asks.

"We've talked. I don't know if I'm ready to really define what we are right now. I will, though. I want to be more than just sure, you know?"

He heads to the shop door since we're about to open. "Yeah, I know."

Sam is right; getting serious is not my thing. I'm cautious, and the fortress I've built hasn't been penetrated yet, so if Maddie is already scaling some walls, then I need to make sure I'm ready if I plan on surrendering completely.

CHAPTER 24

Maddie

The day has flown by, with a steady stream of emails, phone calls, and interactions with the guests we are currently having staying here. I haven't had much time to think of anything else until now.

I grab a mug from the cabinet to pour myself a cup of hot tea. As I wait for the whistle of the kettle to signal the water is done heating up, I look out the back window. My mind drifts to the last month and a half, but specifically the last couple of days.

I think about all that has happened between me and Ryder since we shared a picnic near that giant oak tree by my cottage. Confessions of developing feelings. Conversations about our past. Shared moments full of laughter and intimacy. A kind of intimacy that you can't just find with anyone.

Every moment is full of trust and genuine care.

I'm so lost in thought that when the whistle echoes

around me, I'm startled. Rolling my eyes at myself, I remove the kettle from the burner, pour the water into my cup, and place my tea bag in the water, allowing it to steep.

"Is there enough water for two?" The question comes from behind me. When I turn to the familiar voice, Evelyn is walking through the kitchen doorway.

I give her a smile in greeting. "Of course, I'll grab you a cup." Pulling another mug from the cabinet, I prepare a second cup.

"My day has been so busy with tedious tasks. How was your day?" she asks as she accepts the cup of tea from me. "Thank you."

"Mine too. We had at least eight new reservation requests today alone," I say as we both make our way over the table and take a seat.

"Well, I guess we can't complain about that. I think the ad you suggested really helped get us noticed," she says.

I blow on my tea before I take a small sip. "I agree on both accounts, especially now that we're reaching the end of summer. Soon, it will be fall, and the holidays will be here before we know it. Do you find we're busy during that time?"

"It's different every year. Are you thinking you'll want to go home for the holidays to see your family?"

Releasing a quiet sigh, I shrug my shoulders. "I'm really not sure what my plans will be. I haven't ever been away from home for the holidays." I blow on my tea again.

"Is it this budding relationship with Ryder that has you hesitating?"

I look up quickly, startled by her direct question.

169

"I didn't really think about that. Honestly, I haven't thought about it at all until now."

I can't decide if that answer is a lie. Maybe it is because of Ryder, but maybe it's not. Evelyn remains quiet and sips her tea. I do the same, and after a few minutes, she speaks up again. "You know, it's none of my business, but I love Ryder. And I've come to care about you truly. You're quickly becoming family."

"I feel the same about you and Henry, and, of course, I know you love Ryder."

"The reason I say this is I can see the way you watch each other when the other one isn't looking. I've noticed since the day you got here. And Ryder isn't always so free with his feelings."

"I could never hurt him."

She reaches across the table and pats my hand. "Oh, Madelyn. I know that. And I don't think he would ever want to hurt you. I worry it may happen regardless. So, I'm saying it out loud to you just as Henry and I said it to Ryder yesterday afternoon when he came up here after dropping you off. Take care of one another. Be certain about every step you take, but also just let things happen. Your hearts will know, I promise."

"Thank you for saying all of this and for caring so much. Everyone seems to keep telling me to listen to my heart. I can only say I'm trying, and so far, I'm listening as best I can."

"Trying with the best intentions is a good place to start," Evelyn says. "Especially because there are no guarantees in life when it comes to love."

"And isn't that just the scariest part?" I confide in her. "Just know that I'm doing my best to live in the moment while also protecting both mine and Ryder's hearts."

"And that is all we can ask," she says and then takes another long drink of her tea. "There's nothing like a good afternoon tea."

"I couldn't agree more," I say, and just like that, we fall into a completely different conversation. I really appreciate the way both Evelyn and Henry are so naturally protective but also don't judge. It's no wonder Ryder turned into such a thoughtful and deliberate man.

"Hey, Gran! Hey, Maddie!" Rosalind greets us as she walks into the kitchen.

"Well, hello, Rosalind, honey. How was everything with school today? Did you get your project turned in to your professor?" Evelyn asks, standing up and giving her granddaughter a hug.

"School was good, and my assignment is all turned in. It was such a relief," Ros says.

"I'm glad. Are you hungry?"

"I am," Henry chirps from the doorway he just walked through as Ros responds with a simple, "No, thank you."

"Of course, you're hungry. You're always hungry," Evelyn responds.

I sit and watch them interact with each other while I finish my tea. It's just so normal, and it feels good to be around them.

It brings a smile to my face when she immediately starts making a snack for Henry. He leans in and places a sweet peck on Evelyn's cheek. It was such a natural display of thanks between two people in love.

"So, Maddie, Grandad reminded me yesterday we all met when we were kids. I think it's sweet that Ryder has finally gotten the chance to act on his crush on you." She laughs, and so do Evelyn and Henry.

"His crush on me?"

"Oh, yeah, I can remember he practically cried when our mom and dad wouldn't let us stay one more night. They thought it was because he didn't want to leave Gran and Grandad, but I heard him ask Grandad at least three times when you were coming back. I may have been ten, but I wasn't stupid."

"Huh, his crush on me." I can't help the grin that spreads across my face. "That's cute. I'm pretty sure I had a crush on him, too. I can remember being so sad that he was gone by the time my grandparents and I got back here."

"What a coincidence. All these years and now look," she says.

"Yeah, what a coincidence," I repeat.

"I think it's sweet," Evelyn says.

"God has a way, doesn't he?" Henry adds.

Just about that time, my phone chimes with a text message.

> Ryder: Hey gorgeous, I hope your day has gone well. Say you'll stay with me again tonight?

Reading his words, I can't help the reaction it elicits or the smile it puts on my face. Is another night too much? Suddenly, I hear Caro and Evelyn's words in my mind: "Listen to your heart; it will know."

Ryder: I'm sorry. Maybe it's too much. Forget I said anything.

Me: No. I mean, no to it being too much, and yes, to staying with you.

Ryder: You just made my whole day…my whole night! I'll swing by later and pick you up.

"That must be some text with that look on your face," Ros says, raising her eyebrows.

"Rosalind, leave Maddie alone," Evelyn tells her and goes back to writing down some things in her calendar. Henry is sitting quietly at the end of the table, eating his snack and reading the paper.

"It's your brother," I state before going back to the text message.

"I assumed," she says.

I have different plans than Ryder coming to get me.

Me: Don't worry about coming to get me. I will grab a bag; then I think I want to walk. It's a nice day, and I feel like moving my legs. See you in a bit.

Ryder: If that is what you want, I will see you a little later.

Me: See you later.

I put my phone in my pocket and take my cup over to the sink to wash out. Once I'm done, I dry my hands and turn to the others. Henry is still reading his paper. Evelyn is now planning the upcoming week's menu. And Rosalind is busy doing some homework with a textbook open.

"Okay, I'm off to answer some more emails and check

in with the guest one last time before I head out. Do you need me to do anything else before I leave for the day?"

Evelyn looks up from her notebook. "No, I think we're all good. Will you be having dinner with Ryder tonight?"

"Yes, I'm going to walk into town and meet him after I stop at the market."

"Then I won't expect you for dinner. Be sure to give that grandson of mine a hug for me."

"Will do. And I will make sure to say goodbye before I head home for the day."

I make my way to my office and glance at my watch to check the time. I have about an hour's worth of work left, which is perfect timing for meeting Ryder just before he closes up shop for the day.

Taking a seat at my desk, I try to focus on my work instead of another night with Ryder.

• • •

I was able to finish my work surprisingly quickly. Once I shut everything down, I said my goodbyes and walked back to my cottage to throw a few things in a bag. Now, I'm ambling down the street into town. As I walk down the street, I pay attention to the feel of the crisp air and all my surroundings. It's part of what I find charming about living here. I'm used to nature that comes with heat and humidity, and while I love that, this cool, dry air feels fantastic. I'm beginning to love these new surroundings.

As I approached the main street, I began to see more and more people out and about. Tourists, no doubt, milled about the main drag, moving in and out of the local shops. I'm still struck by the quaintness of this town and the way it fits perfectly nestled against the hills.

When I arrive at the market, I run in and grab a few things so I can make dinner tonight for me and Ryder. It didn't take me long, and then I made my way down the street in the direction of Ryder's shop. As I pass Dream Bean Cafe, I peer in through the window to see if Molly is working. She happens to be looking out the front window at the same time and spots me. We wave at one another, and it seems as if she might wave me in, but a customer walks up to the counter and captures her regard.

I considered going inside and grabbing a chai latte, but when I glanced at my watch, I decided against it since Ryder would be off soon.

Instead, I continue down the sidewalk until I reach the shop. As I walked up, I noticed that the large garage door was open, so I walked to the edge and peeked inside. There's a car being worked on by a younger guy with blonde shaggy hair.

"Excuse me," I say, and he looks over at the sound of my voice. When our eyes meet, I smile, and he grins back. "Hi, sorry to bother you. I'm looking for Ryder."

"Oh, yeah, you must be Maddie. I can get him for you. I think he might be in the office."

My smile widens at the way he spits it out in rapid succession.

"Yes, I'm Maddie. And you are?"

"Yeah, I'm Billy," he says as he walks toward me, his hand extended.

I look down at his hand when he gets close enough. He must notice the slight grimace on my face because he quickly pulls his hand away.

"Shit, I'm sorry, I forgot how dirty my hands are," he says, an apologetic look on his face.

"No problem," I reassure him.

"Anyway, I'll go let Ryder know you're here."

"No need, I'm here," a voice says from a doorway at the back of the shop.

A second later, Ryder's handsome face comes into view. When he sees me, a grin forms on his face. "Hey there, I just finished up. Have you been here long?"

Shaking my head, I say, "Nope, Billy and I just introduced ourselves."

Ryder glances in Billy's direction, who is still standing next to me, silently allowing Ryder and me to chat back and forth. "Oh, were you?" Ryder asks, now making eye contact with Billy.

"Well, yeah, uh…it was nice meeting you, Maddie. You want me to close up, boss?"

Ryder keeps his face serious, "Yes, and don't forget to check every door. See you in the morning."

"It was nice meeting you, too, Billy," I say as Billy walks away. He looks over his shoulder and flashes me a quick smile.

Ryder shakes his head and walks over to me, taking me by the hand, but only after he takes my overnight bag from me. Leading me around the building, he says, "That kid was around you, what, three minutes? And he was smitten."

"Oh, stop. Now you're just being silly."

"I don't think so, gorgeous. I could see it in his eyes."

"He seems like a sweetheart. Has he worked for you long?"

"A while. Sam and I took him under our wing. We're trying to teach him some responsibility. He already has a natural hand with mechanics."

"That's good of you both to do that for him."

"Well, we need someone, and Billy has the potential. Not to mention, he has the drive, so it works out for all of us." He leads me up the stairs to his apartment. "What do you have there in that grocery bag?"

"Oh, I was thinking of making dinner."

"Thank God! I was hoping you were going to say that," he says. "I was worrying a little about what I had in my fridge."

"You will never have to worry about not having a meal when I'm around because I'm always thinking about food." I grin from ear to ear.

We reach the top of the steps, and Ryder unlocks the door for us, then takes the grocery bag from me, leaving me empty-handed.

"Thank you, sir."

"You're welcome, madam."

Ryder places the grocery bag on the counter, then walks over to his bedroom area and puts my overnight bag on the bench at the end of his bed.

"If you don't mind, I'm going to take a quick shower, then I would be happy to help with dinner. Make yourself at home."

"Thanks, I don't mind getting started. Go ahead and do your thing. I think I know my way around this kitchen after the other night."

"Cool," he says as he walks over and places a soft kiss on my cheek.

"Cool," I say back.

Ryder closes the door to the bathroom behind him. I kick off my shoes and get started on dinner, thinking to myself the entire time how nice this feels. It was so nice, in fact, that I could easily get used to it.

CHAPTER 25

Maddie

It's been a little over two months since the first night Ryder and I spent together, and it's easier to count how many nights I've slept alone since then than it is to count the ones I've spent with him. We've bounced back and forth between one another's homes with ease. It has become natural, and honestly, I hate the nights we don't spend together.

I've never been happier, and as far as I can tell, Ryder is happy, too.

"You ready for our little nature adventure?"

I turn when I hear his voice as he walks into the room. It's Sunday, and we're both off.

"Yep," I say as I tie my shoes. "I knew my hiking shoes were going to come in handy."

"Good, the trail is super long, and it loops around, but when you get close to the summit, it does get a little steep."

I stand and wrap my arms around him. "Have no fear.

I can handle myself." I give him a long, slow kiss before I pull back so we can get on our way.

"I have no doubt you're capable."

I laugh, "I'm not sure what you're insinuating, but I know you don't just mean my hiking skills."

Ryder grabs our backpacks and opens the door.

"You're smart, too. Now, let's get out of here so we can enjoy our day and make it to Gran and Grandad's for dinner."

"I'm right behind you." I follow Ryder out the door.

And before I know it, we're flying down the highway with the radio blasting.

"What's this place called again?"

"Quarry and Park Ridge Trail Loop. You're going to be amazed when you see the view from the top."

"I can only imagine. Do you think we're dressed warm enough?"

"Absolutely, we should be totally fine."

We ride the remainder of the drive in silence. Ryder reaches over and takes my hand in his, linking our fingers together, and I look over at him with a smile. I watch as the ocean, hills, and coastline pass by.

When we arrive, Ryder easily finds a spot to park, which he's surprised by since parking is usually limited at this end of the trail. We're starting on the Park Ridge end. Ryder told me he felt like I would enjoy it since it runs through farmland.

We grab our bags, which we each packed with plenty of water and a picnic lunch, and head for the trailhead.

"Ready?" he asks.

"Ready!" I say with genuine enthusiasm.

Together, we begin our trek up to the summit.

• • •

Ryder

We're about forty minutes into the short hike to the summit, and I'm not at all surprised to find Maddie moving swiftly. She seemed to be enjoying the adrenaline the terrain was evoking in her. I wanted us to do something outdoorsy for multiple reasons, but especially since I heard her talking to her brother the other night. She told him that she feeds off nature, but she really hasn't taken the time to enjoy and immerse herself in all it has to offer around us. Top that with the fact that I love hiking and the outdoors myself. I thought, why not take her to one of my favorite spots? It's close and short, the perfect fun adventure.

"This is so beautiful. Thank you for bringing me here," she says, interrupting my thoughts.

I look in her direction a few feet to my left, and she is beaming at me from ear to ear.

"You're welcome, but if you think this is the beautiful part, then I can't wait to see what you are going to think when we get to the top.

"I can't even imagine."

"No, I don't think you can until you actually see it."

We continued on for another fifteen minutes, and as we came to the summit, I took Maddie's hand to guide her around some rocks we came upon. We walk hand in hand until we reach the top, and I hear a slight gasp slip from between her lips.

"I'm speechless."

Maddie spins in a small circle, taking in the spectacular view.

"Told ya," I say, loving the look of awe on her face.

"I've never seen anything like this before. I mean, we can literally see where the ocean meets the horizon. And, in the direction, what is that town?"

"That's San Luis Obispo."

"Thank you again. This is amazing."

"Thank you for coming with me. It's been a while since I've been here."

I watch as she pulls out her phone and snaps some pictures. She even talks me into a selfie or two.

"Are you hungry?" I ask her. We brought a small picnic of food.

"Actually, I could eat something."

We find a spot where we can picnic, and I lay the blanket down we brought. Maddie starts pulling out the snacks, and we relax, taking in our surroundings.

"You're right; that was the perfect hike for a day where time is a bit limited," Maddie says before biting into the cheese and crackers she stacked together.

"It really is. I'm glad we came."

She looks out over the horizon. "Me, too."

"Gran will be glad we'll still make it back in time to have Sunday dinner."

"I know; I love how important it is to her and how

she's invited me into the tradition."

"She's pretty special like that; always able to make sure everyone feels loved and included."

"It reminds me of my own grandmother and helps ease some of the homesickness I feel for my family."

Maddie looks away wistfully, and I can feel her sadness at the loss of time with her family. I know it can't always be easy for her. But she seems happy despite missing them. It does make me wonder how long she'll be here, though. How long will I have her? Can she stay indefinitely? And if she can't, how do I feel about that possibility?

I sit here, watching her and thinking of how she's become such an intricate part of my daily life. We've fallen into such an easy rhythm when we are together. Honestly, I can't remember ever enjoying just being with anyone as much as Maddie.

"Earth to Ryder."

Her voice pulls me from my thoughts.

"Sorry, I drifted a bit into another world. What were you saying?"

"No worries, everything okay?"

"Yep, just thinking."

"Good, I was just asking how long before we head back down?"

Glancing at my watch, I see we've already been up here for about thirty minutes.

"We can pack up and head back down now if you're ready."

"While I don't think I will ever get tired of this view, I know we should get going so we can clean up and be on time for supper."

"Being late for Gran's Sunday meals is never an option," I laugh.

Maddie grins, nodding her head. "No doubt. She has made that very clear."

We both laugh at the thought of my grandmother's stern but loving expectations. Maddie and I begin packing things up so we can be on our way.

She talks me into one more selfie, and as she takes the picture, her lips press against my cheek. There is a warm feeling that sits in my chest at the gesture—a natural, genuine feeling of happiness, and also a sudden fear of it disappearing.

CHAPTER 26

Ryder

I hear the shower turn off as my eyes slowly open, the morning light shining through the blinds of Maddie's room. I stretch my body out while I lie in bed. As she walks through the bathroom door with a towel wrapped around her, I can't help admiring the round curve of her breast peeking above the towel's edge.

Propping myself up on one elbow, I say, "You're gorgeous."

She grins and stands facing me. "And you're sweet."

"I don't know if I would call what I'm thinking about doing to you sweet."

"Oh well, maybe I should give you a chance to show me so I can decide for myself," Maddie says as she allows her towel to drop to the floor, revealing her bare skin glistening from the dampness of her shower. "Or better yet, maybe I will show you the things I want to do to you."

She casually crawls onto the bed, gently pushes me

down, and climbs over me until she's straddling me. Maddie leans forward, slowly peppering kisses across my chest. Eventually, she moves up my neck and keeps going until her lips are set perfectly against my lips. She pauses when we're mouth to mouth. I open my eyes to find her gaze looking directly into mine. Neither of us moves; we don't say a word, and our only communication is through our eyes. She is trusting me with her body. Her heart. And I can see how hard she's working at opening up the gate of the wall she's built around herself. I'm trying to convey the same message to her. And I hope to God she can see how much I'm giving her.

After that moment, we continued to savor the feeling of one another and then moved with a little more fever. She rocks her hips a little against mine as we take our kiss deeper. I wrap my arms a little tighter around her. I pull my mouth from hers, and as I place my hand around her breast, my lips close around her nipple, causing Maddie to whimper and moan.

"Ryder, my God."

The desire I hear in her voice pushes me to take more of what I want. I move to her other breast, and her hips press forward to grind down against mine. With each forward movement, I get harder, making it more challenging to savor Maddie before taking her completely.

"I need to be inside you, Maddie."

She reaches over to the side table for protection and swiftly eases it on before lifting it until she is centered over me. Gently, Maddie inches down until I'm entirely sheathed by her. I can't help each moan that escapes me, all the while watching Maddie's face full of satisfaction.

"I needed you, too," she says, then begins moving on top of me and, swirling her hips and rolling them against mine. I move beneath her in sync with every move she makes. She moans. I moan. Being inside of her, connected with her in this way, is the sweetest intimacy I've ever experienced.

I'm so overwhelmed with the emotions I'm feeling and the things I want to say to her. Explain to her. But for now, all I can do is show her with every caress and movement inside her. I hope she understands what I'm trying to convey.

Together, we move and touch until we both fall apart. Maddie collapses against my chest, and I welcome her with open arms, cradling her into me and holding on for dear life. My heart races with the sudden feeling of what it would be like to lose her. I don't say a word. I just let that dread settle deep into my gut, praying it is so far down that it will never come back to the light.

Pulling Maddie even closer to me, I listen to her breathing and allow it to lull me back to sleep.

• • •

"Grandad, how did you know Gran was the one?" I ask as I help him load some wood into the back of his small Chevy pickup truck.

"Ry, I knew from the moment I laid my eyes on her that she was going to change my life, so I guess it was right then."

I pick up another few logs and stack them next to the ones Grandad just laid down. One of the most comforting things about my grandparents is they are both still so capable. I'd be lying if I said I never worried about them. Considering his words, I continue to work. I'm not sure if that was the answer I was looking for or if it helped ease my mind when it came to Madelyn.

Before I can fully process it or say anything else, Grandad continues, "But that isn't the question you should be asking yourself, kid."

As I reach for a few more logs, I freeze at his words. I stand up instead and look over at him. I find him watching me. "You hear what I'm saying? You're asking yourself the wrong question. In all honesty, most men do when it comes to women and relationships." He walks over to me, pats my shoulder, and then proceeds to move some more wood to the truck.

He smiles as he passes me because I'm still staring at him. I heard him, but I'm trying to piece together exactly what he's saying.

"And what question is that?" I say by the time he's already heading back toward me with another armload.

When he reaches my side, he stops and looks me directly in the eyes. "Are you the one for her? Because if you aren't, then she isn't the one for you. Suppose you don't put her feelings first. If you don't think about how you can make her life better with each new sunrise, then you aren't the one. Especially if you don't want to make those your priorities, but if every breath you've taken since you met her is for her and her alone, then I believe that answers that fundamental question. Because that is what she deserves… all your breaths."

Henry Evans has proven every day of my life that he is a true gentleman. He is everything I've ever wanted to be, and I now understand just where my father's passion for my mother came from. His dad, my grandfather, showed us not only love but also how to love.

"Grandad, I love you. Thank you for everything." I lean in, and he welcomes me into a hug.

"I love you, too, Ryder. Now make sure you remember your worth in all of this and that Maddie is worthy of the best."

We pull apart, and Grandad says, "Let's finish loading this wood so we can get it inside the house and have some lunch. Your grandmother promised sandwiches and soup if we took care of this before lunchtime."

Doing what he says, I begin to work again. "If you don't move a little faster, then we're not getting that lunch," I tease.

"You better watch it, kid. I can make sure that you get dish duty for Sunday dinners for a month straight if you don't watch yourself."

"Mouth shut," I shout over my shoulder as I pass him.

"That's what I thought."

We continued to work until it was all loaded into the truck bed, then we headed up to the house and started unloading it into all the rooms with fireplaces. We finish up by placing the remaining wood in his weatherproof storage bin. There are some colder days coming up, and my grandparents want to be prepared. I'm always glad to be able to help them out with things like this when they need it.

Once we finish up, we head inside, and all I can think about is whether or not Maddie is going to be able to have lunch with us, too.

Every breath? Yeah, I think I know my answer to that question.

CHAPTER 27

Maddie

My day at the bed and breakfast was short and uneventful. We are between guests, and I breezed through my booking emails. I was able to get everything on the calendar and reply to all the inquiries that came in over the last couple of days.

"Hey, Molly!" I say as I walk into the coffee shop. I need a little pick-me-up. Although my day wasn't busy, the night before was a late one.

"Maddie, it's been days!"

She makes her way around the counter until she's standing in front of me.

"I know, our days have been full. How has business been? School?"

"Eww, school is the usual. Boring. And mostly, pointless," she says, scrunching her nose up before continuing. "And business has been good. My sister refuses to help out, which is pretty lame. I can't understand why, at fourteen years old, I'm more reliable than my seventeen-year-old sister, but whatever. She's such a loser, and my parents are such pushovers."

I laugh because I can remember feeling this way on more than one occasion when it came to Caroline and Jake when we were younger.

"Yeah, well, that's siblings for you. As for your parents, cut them a little slack. They're probably doing their best juggling you, your sister, and this business."

"You're probably right. Anywho, did you want a latte?"

"Yes, the biggest size you have, please."

Molly walks around to the other side of the counter. I realize now I'm the only customer in here. It's no wonder Molly spoke so freely about her annoyance with her family. If anyone else had been in there, Molly's parents would have known what she said within the hour.

"So, you and Ryder are serious, huh?"

I almost laugh because she doesn't beat around the bush. She's fearless, and I love it.

"Me and Ryder, serious? Yeah, I guess we just might be."

In all these months, we've kept it as low-key as possible, so we really haven't said much to anyone. We definitely haven't defined what's happening between us. All I know is I want to be with him as much as I can.

"Might? You mean, you haven't talked about it?"

And there she goes again, straight to the point.

"Not really. We've just let it happen the way it's happening."

"You'll have to talk about it soon. Even I know this."

"You're probably right."

"I know."

This time, I do laugh out loud. Molly never disappoints when it comes to entertaining conversations. I'm so glad I met her when I first got to town. She handed me my latte over the counter, and I placed my money on the counter before taking the drink. I hear the bell of the door chime, indicating a new customer has entered the shop.

"Well, thanks for the pick me up. I'll see you later."

"No problem, Maddie. See ya."

As I walk out of the door, my conversation with Molly plays over in my head. Although Ryder and I's relationship has developed over time, we haven't talked about where our feelings stand at this point. And that worries me.

When I was talking to Caroline the other day about my worries, she told me to let it go. And if I couldn't, then I should say something to him. She asked me why Ryder had to be the one to bring up a discussion about where our relationship was going. She also wanted to know why it mattered because it seemed that if we were staying at each other's place nearly every night, then it's likely we'd be on the same page. I reminded her that if that meant anything, then Connor and I would still be together.

So, I waited three days, and then some, after my conversation with Caro, to see if I could let it go and not worry so much. But I guess it might be time for me to be honest with him about how I'm feeling. And take a chance on whether or not my feelings are reciprocated.

• • •

Ryder called earlier to let me know he left his apartment door unlocked for me and that I should go in and make myself at home. I've definitely grown more comfortable letting myself in and being at his place alone. Ryder often leaves the door open for me, and I've spent enough nights here that it's starting to feel very familiar.

When I enter the apartment, I walk over to the bed and put my bag down. I stopped bringing my own toiletries because Ryder has given me a toothbrush and all the things I need. I did the same for him at my house. It seemed silly for us to keep packing those things every time, not to mention we often didn't plan where we'd be staying.

Glancing at my watch, I see it's four o'clock, which means Ryder will probably be up here any minute. I walk over to the couch, switching the television on. Just as I'm kicking my shoes off, my phone rings. I look down at it as I grab my latte. It's Caroline.

"Caro, what's shakin'?"

"Madds," I can hear the tears in her voice.

It alarms me, so I sit up and put my cup down.

"Caro, what's wrong? Rob? The kids? Is everything okay?" I ask her, panicked.

"Yeah...yeah, they're fine. Uh, it's..."

Dread builds in my chest. I didn't want to say it, but she was not talking fast enough, so I interrupted her.

"Oh, God, is it Mama? Daddy?"

"Maddie, stop! Mama and Daddy are fine, too. It's Jake. He's uh...he's..."

"Jake? What's wrong with Jake, Caro?"

I'm standing now and pacing back and forth in front of the couch.

"He's been in a bad accident, Madds. He hasn't woken up. They haven't told us much, but it's not looking good for him, Madds. Mama is a mess. Daddy is holding it together for her, but I can see he is just as much of a mess as she is."

I feel like I might puke. My knees feel weak. Just then, Ryder walks through the door.

"I'm home. Where's my..." he calls out.

The moment our eyes meet, I can't hold myself up anymore, and I fall to the floor. Before I can even take another breath, Ryder is at my side, lifting me into his arms. "Maddie? Baby? What's wrong?"

At the sound of his concern for me, I can't hold the tears back. They start to flow. Jake. My parents, they need me. Caroline needs me. Oh, my God, Jake needs me. A sob leaves my body.

"Baby, please tell me what's wrong." Ryder's panic has escalated.

I can tell Caroline is saying something on the other end of the line, but I can barely hear her now.

Ryder pulls the phone from my hand and me against him. He puts the phone on speaker. I can hear Caroline crying.

"Hello...uh, this is Ryder Evans."

"Ryder, this is Rob, Madelyn's brother-in-law. I had to take the phone from my wife; umm, there's been an accident."

"An accident?" Ryder questions.

"Jake, their brother...my brother. He's been a terrible accident. It's pretty serious."

"I see," Ryder gains composure. "What kind of accident? What do I need to do to help Maddie?"

"It was a car accident. We haven't heard much yet."

Something changes in Ryder's breathing, and I put my hand over his heart. He looks down at me and places a kiss on the top of my head.

"I can help get Madelyn on a plane back home. Let me calm her down and get things going. I will let you guys know when she will be there."

"Tell...tell...Caro, I love her. Tell her I'm coming. Tell everyone I'm coming home," I say through my tears.

"I will, Madds. She loves you, too. Uh, thanks, Ryder."

"You're welcome. I'll send you the information soon."

Ryder hangs the phone up. He holds me and soothes me. I feel so safe.

But Jake isn't safe, and I need to be there.

"Will you help me?"

"Of course, I'll do whatever you need me to do."

"I need to go home. I wanna go home."

"I will get you home as soon as I can, I promise."

He holds me a little tighter, and I let him. It feels safe. Being in his arms gives me the feeling that everything will be okay.

"Thank you, Ryder."

"No need to thank me. I'd do anything for you."

CHAPTER 28

Ryder

From the moment I walked in the door and found Maddie dropping to her knees, crying, I was consumed with grief and worry. I realized I couldn't protect her from this pain, but hearing that Jake was in a car accident stirred up emotions in me from the past.

I've heard those words before: *"We aren't certain of the extent of the injuries, but it doesn't look good."* Back then, those words were not meant for my young teenage ears to hear, but I was eavesdropping when the ER doctor told my grandparents the news. I haven't been able to forget those words, and they'll stumble into my thoughts every now and then since that day. The day that changed my life forever.

I can't stand the idea that Maddie could experience a similar loss, but it's not in my control. I know what her family means to her, so I understand what this situation could do to her. The impact will have a ripple effect, and selfishly, I'm even a little worried about what it means for us.

Pushing these thoughts aside, I focus on Maddie and what she needs right now.

It's been at least an hour since she last cried, and I finally got her to eat a little. We're back at her house now, and she's in her room packing. I'm searching the internet for a flight.

"There's a flight at six in the morning out of San Luis Obispo with a layover at LAX before landing in Austin at two in the afternoon. It seems like the best option timewise, but what do you think?" I holler out from the living room.

She doesn't respond, and just when I'm about to get up and check on her, she appears in the opening of the hallway. Her eyes are swollen from all the tears she's shed in the last couple of hours, and her face is etched with worry.

"Did you hear me?"

She nods, "Yeah, that should work. Are you coming with me?"

I sort of freeze for a minute; those feelings of despair start creeping their way back into my mind. "Uh, well, do you want me to?" I ask the question. As it comes out, I can hear the struggle in my voice. The grief from my past and what I fear Maddie might need from me. Am I capable of giving her this kind of support?

"Do you want to?" she asks.

I begin to make excuses. "Won't I be in the way? Not to mention, I need to make sure Sam and Billy can handle the shop." Everything coming out of my mouth sounds lame, even to my ears.

"Oh, uh…you know, you're probably right. I need to focus on Jake and my family."

I don't fight her. It's easier to hide from my grief if I allow both of us to believe our excuses. And Maddie is letting me.

"I'll just need to let Rob and Caro know so they can hopefully pick me up from the airport. If not, I can always take an Uber to the hospital. I don't know who's watching the kids." She pats her pockets, then looks around the room in an almost panic. "I should call them back. See if that works and if there is anything new happening."

Coward, I think.

Again, I pretend I'm only thinking of Maddie. I mean, I am. I'm worried about her. I don't want her to hurt, and that's what matters most. I walk over to her and take her hand just as she's about to turn for her room. She turns back toward me, looking up into my eyes. God, I want to make all of that pain go away. "Maddie, I was just texting with your brother-in-law. There isn't anything new to report with Jake. As for your flight, I will let him know the details, too. He said he would be there to pick you up no matter what time it is."

Again, she nods, and a single tear slips down her cheek. "I feel so helpless," she whispers.

Maddie's feelings are a perfect distraction from my own. I pull her against my chest and hold her, caressing her hair soothingly. "I know you do, but I promise you wouldn't feel any different if you were right next to him and your family. We will get you there as quickly as humanly possible." I place a kiss on top of her head and pull back a little so I can see her face once more. "I'll book that flight for you. Why don't you take a long hot shower? I think it will make you feel a little better."

"You're right. I think I'll do that." Maddie rises up on her toes and places her lips against mine. A soft, sweet, lingering kiss. "Thank you for everything."

"I'd do anything for you. I hope you know that."

She gives me an almost smile. "I do now." Maddie squeezes my hand, and I watch her walk away as she disappears into her room.

Once she's out of sight, I return to the computer and book her flight. I let her sister and brother-in-law know the flight information, and they said to let her know that Rob would be there to pick her up. I go into the kitchen and clean up a few dishes that are in the sink before heading to check on her.

When I walk into the room, Maddie is slipping an oversized cotton T-shirt over her head. I walk up behind her, wrap my arms around her waist, and nestle my face into her neck. Maddie grips my arms with her hands and pulls them tighter around her. She leans back into me, and then she slides her hand to mine and starts moving it downward and doesn't stop until my hand is covering her center. She takes my hand and begins rubbing it against her before she takes my fingers and pushes them inside her. In and out.

"Maddie, are you sure about this? We don't need to do this."

"Touch me, please. I need this. I need you," she begs.

I know she's looking for a distraction. Someone and

something to get lost in, and I hope this is what she needs. I listen to what she's asking for and take more control of my movements. Maddie moans, and so I push deeper inside her. She feels so good. I move and rub against her, coaxing out more whimpers and sounds from between her lips.

Taking my hand, she moves it until she can turn and face me. Our eyes meet, and she begins undressing me, and I allow her to retake control. I can still see the worry lurking in the depths of her gaze, but now there is desire clouding it.

When I'm completely undressed, Maddie takes my hand once more, leading me over the bed. She hands me a condom, then lays back on the bed and spreads open for me. I put on the protection and only hesitate a second to look over her long, lean body before I crawl on top of her.

"I need you inside me."

I push inside her in one swift motion, and both of us sigh in satisfaction. There is no waiting; I push in and out of her in quick motions. She matches me every step of the way. I needed to be inside her as much as she needed me to be. We put every emotion coursing through us into our lovemaking until we are both sated and collapse from exhaustion.

It felt beautiful, full of happiness, but also an undefined sadness lingers between it all. The irony of it is this feels like such a defining moment in our relationship. I don't know what it is, but there's a shift, and something tells me it's all so fragile and precious. I want to hold her and never let go, but she has to go. I know that.

Just as we always do, Maddie lies cradled against me.

We're wrapped up in one another, and it feels like this is how we're supposed to be.

"I'm going to miss you," she says quietly.

This time, it's me who has a tear slipping from my eye. I pull her in tighter.

"I'm going to miss you, too."

And this is how we fall asleep. Holding one another like it could be the last time.

• • •

We're standing outside the airport, embracing one another in a long, clinging hug. This is something I hate about flying these days. I want to stay with her until the very last second before she gets on the plane. But I can't. So, instead, we have to say our goodbyes in a rushed way because this is a no-loitering zone. And all I can think about is loitering.

"I wish I could walk in with you," I tell her.

"Me, too. But we both know that is pointless." She hugged me again, and I could see the traffic control guy eyeing us. "Thank you again, Ryder. For everything."

"I told you. No need to thank me. I would do anything for you."

She nods with a half-smile. "Yeah, I know." Maddie glances at her watch. "Well, I better get going. I'll let you know when I get there."

"Yeah, okay. And let me know what is happening with Jake. Gran and Grandad want updates, too, but I will keep them posted so you don't need to focus on all of us. Just focus on your family."

"Bye, Maddie."

"Goodbye, Ryder."

We both turn. Maddie for the entrance and me to my truck.

I don't make it even one step before I turn back to her. She must have had the same thought because she's coming toward me, too. Suddenly, we're back in each other's arms, and I'm giving her a long, hard kiss. One to last. One to remember. One that will hopefully bring her back when it's time.

A whistle blows, and we pull apart, both grinning and stepping backward in opposite directions.

"Bye," I say again.

"Bye."

I hop in my truck, and this time, I make myself keep my eyes forward on the road ahead of me. I don't want to think about all the negative things trying to creep into my head. Instead, I think about Maddie. That kiss. And how I would give her my very last breath to see her happy.

CHAPTER 29

Maddie

It's been three days since I arrived in Texas. I spent three long days in the hospital in downtown Austin. My parents, sister, and I haven't left. Rob has been in and out often, spending nights with the kids and driving back during the day to bring us things we need.

The other person that has been here practically around the clock is Connor. When I first saw him, I wanted to punch him in the face. But I really didn't have the energy, and he genuinely seemed concerned for Jake and my family. I've managed minimal interaction with him at this point.

Ryder and I have been texting multiple times a day. I haven't heard his voice, though, and I miss it.

But I can't think about myself right now. I have to focus on Jake. He still hasn't woken up. It's been four days, and the longer it goes, the more our level of worry escalates.

"Hey, baby girl, want some coffee?" Mama asks.

It's about seven in the morning. Any sleep we've been able to get has been in chairs and on makeshift pallets on the floor. I'm lying on a small waiting room couch with a blanket wrapped around me.

Looking up at her, I blink to adjust my eyes to the fluorescent lighting. "Uh, yeah…yeah, but I can go get it for us, Mama."

"Madelyn, I need to do something; get up and move so I can stop overthinking. I've got it."

"Okay, then, I'll take one with a little cream."

"I'll be right back. Let your daddy know if he wakes up that I'm grabbing some coffee. He finally dozed off a couple of hours ago, so I don't want to wake him. He needs some rest."

"Okay, Mama."

I watch her walk away. She is the strongest woman I know, and yet she looks worn out and a little lost. I sit up and stretch my arms over my head. Across the room, I can see my dad sleeping in the chair, his head propped up on the wing of the chair and a blanket draped across him. Caroline is in the chair next to him, curled in a ball with her arm stretched out far enough that she's resting one hand on our dad.

Pulling my text messages back up, I scroll through the last few from Ryder. He asks about Jake and the rest of my family. He tells me that Evelyn, Henry, and Ros send their love. He even passes along a message from Molly that she's thinking and praying for me. Ryder talks about everyone else but himself.

When we said goodbye, it felt like he was trying to tell me more.

The night Caro called about Jake, I was going to talk to Ryder. Tell him how I'm feeling and hopefully find out what he was feeling. I keep playing these last months over in my head, and everything points to something big and beautiful between us. Then I remind myself I've made this mistake before, and I feel myself doubting him and everything between us.

Movement from the corner of my eye brings me back to my surroundings. When I look over, it's Caroline walking over.

"Hey," she says.

"Hey."

"Where's Mama?"

"She went to get some coffee."

"I'm glad Daddy is still sleeping. I wish I were."

"In a way, me too," I confess. "But I also want to stay away from the dreams."

"I second that one. Do you think he's gonna come out of this, Madds? I mean, really? Not what you hope, but I mean, your gut. What is it saying?"

"Honestly?"

Caroline nods, her eyes shimmering with tears, matching mine.

"I don't know. My gut isn't telling me a damn thing other than it's out of my hands. I've asked God, but He doesn't seem to be answering. I do know that we're supposed to trust Him, though. God wants us to have faith, and if it's His will, Jake will pull through this and wreak havoc on Mama and Daddy's nerves once again."

"God, I hope so."

"Me, too," we hear from behind us. When we turn around, Mama is standing there with a tray of coffee in her hands.

Caroline and I both stand, rushing to take the tray from her. I accept the coffee, and Caro takes Mama by the arm, leading her to a seat.

"I'd take the worry and annoyance and all the trouble your brother has caused over the years until the day I die if God would just let him wake up and come home with us."

"We know, Mama. We know."

"Then I may kill him later for putting all of us through this situation," she says.

We all laugh. I'm not sure if it's the lack of sleep or what, but we all laugh so hard and loud that Daddy sits up with a start.

"What the heck are you girls doing?"

"Oh, John, calm down. We're trying to find light in the darkness."

"Any news yet this morning? What time is it anyway?" Daddy asks.

"It's only about seven thirty. The doctor isn't due here until eight, and visiting starts about eight thirty."

"Is that coffee I smell?

Mama stands up and starts handing coffee out to each of us. "Sure is."

"Thank you, hon," my daddy says as he takes the insulated cup from my mama.

We all sit around chatting, trying desperately to occupy

our minds until the doctor shows up to give us some update on Jake.

Once again, we hear footsteps behind us, and when we all jump up in hopes it's the doctor with some good news, we find Rob and Connor walking around the corner.

My heart sinks. Connor.

Caroline goes up to Rob and wraps her arms around his neck. He reciprocates and gives her a kiss. When I glance in Connor's direction, he's staring directly at me. I nod at him and turn my attention back to my brother-in-law.

"Any news?" Rob asks.

"Not yet. We thought y'all might be the doctor when we heard you coming down the corridor."

"Sorry about that," Rob says. "I ran into Connor in the parking lot, so we came in together." He is looking directly at me when he says this, and since he's standing a step behind Connor, he mouths an apology at me.

I give him a smirk and shake my head to indicate that he has nothing to be sorry for.

Mama turns to Connor. "Connor, it's sweet of you to come visit again, especially so early." She gives him a hug, and he hugs her back.

It's something I've seen them do hundreds of times, but it feels strange now. I can't understand why he keeps coming around. He's been here every day since the accident. He hasn't really tried to speak to me directly, but he hasn't ignored me either. He acknowledges me and has asked me a few questions here and there, but nothing more than surface-level questions.

"I know, but Jake is like family, too. I want to help in

any way I can. You're all like my second family."

Caroline looks at him in disgust, then glances at me and rolls her eyes. It's almost like she is reading my mind and acting out my feelings. I would cause a scene and put him in his place any other time, but one, I don't have the energy, and two, this isn't about us. It's about Jake.

"That's kind but unnecessary," my dad says. I can read the look on his face. Even in this situation, he is worrying about me and how I'm feeling about having Connor around.

I notice Connor flinch. I feel the need to speak up to ease the emotions in the room.

"Regardless, we appreciate it, Connor. Truly. I know Jake would be grateful," I say.

Dad gives me a look, and I give it right back. He shouldn't be thinking about how Connor's presence is making me feel. Especially when I can't even decide what exactly it is that I am feeling.

Connor's head whips in my direction. A look of relief and hope, maybe, covers his features. "Thanks. Can I get anyone anything?"

We all shake our heads. My parents walk to the nurses' station to check on the doctor's timing. Caroline and Rob huddle together, and he fills her in on the morning with the kids. I take a seat and smile when I see a text from Ryder. Once again, he asked me some questions about what was happening with Jake, and then he asked if he could call me at some point.

As I type out a response, I notice Connor staring at me again. I try to ignore him and focus on sending this text message to Ryder.

This all feels awkward, and I may regret making Connor feel so welcome.

• • •

The doctor finally arrived, giving my parents an update. Unfortunately, not much has changed other than the swelling in Jake's brain has gone down significantly.

I decided to go to the cafeteria to grab something I might be able to get down since my appetite has been almost non-existent since I got here.

As I come around the corner, I run directly into Connor and trip. He catches me by the arm and helps keep me upright.

"Sorry...sorry, I was just waiting to talk to you," he says, still holding my arm.

I pull it away and take a step back.

"Connor?"

"I just wanted to talk to you in private for a minute."

"I don't think this is the time or the place."

"I know...I know, but it will only take a couple of minutes. I'll say what I need to say, and then we can go back to your family."

I look around the corridor and then back at him. I feel nervous and uneasy. I hate this feeling. But he's leaving me no choice.

"Fine, what do you need to say that you haven't already said?"

He runs his hand through his hair nervously and sighs.

"I'm sorry."

"Connor, you've said that before."

"Yeah, I know. But I'm really sorry. I ruined every-thing. I ruined our future. And I ruined our friendship."

I want to strangle him. He has the nerve to say this to me now. Finally, he admits that he was wrong. And make assumptions that my whole life was about him. Ruin my future? Maybe I thought that once upon a time, but the funny thing is now I don't. I take a deep breath and think carefully about how to respond. He's obviously waiting for me to because he hasn't said more.

"Well, you're right. You are the one who ruined so much. But I forgive you. I've learned that life is too short to hold onto all the pain and negativity you put on me."

"You forgive me?"

"Yeah, I do," I say, surprising even myself. "So, are we cool now? Or do you have something more that you want to say?"

He stares at me with a slightly confused look on his face, but it eventually morphs into a smile. "No, no. Noth-ing more to say right now. Thanks, Maddie. Your forgive-ness is everything."

We walked back to where my family was still waiting and took turns going in to visit Jake's bedside. For me, that conversation with Connor felt like closure. And my mind drifts to Ryder and everything I miss about him.

CHAPTER 30

Ryder

Five days. It's been five days since Maddie got on a plane back to Texas. And these have been five of the longest days that I can remember. I miss her. It's unbelievable, but I got used to having her next to me when I sleep. I miss our middle-of-the-night snuggles and early-morning lovemaking. Let's be honest: I crave the feeling I get when I catch her looking at me while we're watching television together. Or how the sound of her laughter wraps around me like a warm hug.

Basically, I feel a little empty without her.

I came over to Gran and Grandad's to have dinner with them tonight. I'm pretty sure they've noticed I haven't been myself since Maddie left, and that's the reason for their dinner invitation tonight.

I've contemplated flying out to Texas to be with her and give her some support. We've had lots of text conversations, and she seems so distant and tired. I want to talk to her first and see where she's at with everything. I don't want to be another burden to her. I can't help wondering if she would even want me there. Even if she asked me to come with her, I rejected the idea. I've struggled with that decision. Especially when I think back to my conversation with Grandad the other day; he told me I had to put Maddie before myself. Her feelings had to be my priority. I tripped up a little by not going with her. I need to fix this.

I sit on the front porch swing of the bed and breakfast and dial her number, hoping this is an excellent time to call. As I wait for her to answer, I think about how I'm going to present the idea of flying out. I guess I can't be sure she even wants me there.

The phone rings for the fourth time and then cuts to Maddie's voicemail. To say I'm disappointed is an understatement, but how can I be upset when I know she has so many more important things going on?

I wait for the beep so I can leave a message:

"Hey, it's me, Ryder. I wanted to check in with you and hear your voice. I'm sure you're at the hospital, and being there twenty-four-seven is probably chaotic. We'll talk soon. 'kay. Bye."

I end the call just about the time Grandad sticks his head out the front door and lets me know dinner is ready. I walk into the house behind him, following him into the kitchen. The table is set, and Gran is already sitting down. Grandad and I take a seat.

"Rosalind isn't joining us tonight?" I ask as I pour myself some water.

"She had some homework to get done, but we also

wanted just to have some time with you," Gran says.

We all pass the dishes around and serve ourselves help-ings of everything. Tonight's dinner is baked chicken, and it smells delicious.

"I see. And are we having alone time for any particular reason?"

Grandad and Gran briefly glance at one another and try looking away before I notice. I notice and have to hold back the smile that wants to spread across my face.

"Do we need a particular reason?" Grandad asks, then reaches for mine and Gran's hands so he can lead us in grace.

"Not at all," I say before he starts the prayer.

Once we are done saying grace, we all dig in. We're all silent at first. I would like to say it was because we were enjoying the meal, but in reality, I'm quiet because my mind is playing out every scenario about going to Texas. And I think my grandparents want to discuss something with me that they feel might be a little bit of a touchy sub-ject. My guess is that their subject also involves the same auburn-haired beauty.

When my eyes drift up and across the table, I find them both looking at me. "Alright, you two. What's on your mind?"

"I'm…we're wondering if you've ever figured out the answer to that question we discussed a week or so ago," my grandad asks.

"As a matter of fact, I have, but right now, I'm wonder-ing if what I decided even matters."

Gran almost shouts, like she can't hold back any longer, "Of course, it matters!"

"Maybe. If there's one thing I've learned about Madelyn since we met, it's that her family is everything to her. If they need her or if she feels like they need her, then Maddie is going to do whatever makes them happy, even if it means putting aside her own desires."

"Ry, she deserves you to give her a chance to tell you that herself," Grandad says.

"Your grandfather is right; Madelyn came here a little lost, and she seemed to find something in you. You found something in her, and that alone gives me a reason to encourage you. You deserve happiness, too, Ryder. And we've never seen you happier than you were with her."

I take a deep breath. There's that feeling of fear again, settling into the pit of my stomach. "But what if she's gone back, and now she sees things differently? I already felt a shift when she got that phone call about her brother."

"You aren't being fair, and that's not like you. You're always fair, especially when it comes to other people's emotions. Ryder, she may lose her brother, and you yourself said her family is everything. It was grief preoccupation. You've been there. Your grandfather and I have been there. But it isn't where a person stays when they have someone who loves them through it."

"You said you found the answer to that question, Ry. If you truly did, then you're the person who now needs to love her through this, whatever happens with her family. I get it; taking a chance on love is scary. But she deserves the opportunity to tell you if you're her answer to that same question. Don't hide in the past when the future

215

is so bright."

None of us speak for the rest of the meal. They allow me to sit with my thoughts. They said all they needed to say, and now, it's my job to put it all together. It doesn't take me long to decide what I want and what I need to do.

As Gran places dessert on the table, I say, "Grandad, do you think you can take me to the airport tomorrow?"

Gran claps her hands together with a huge grin. Grandad slaps his hand down on the table. Both are a little excited, and it makes me laugh.

"You bet I can!"

So, it looks like I will be flying to Texas tomorrow. I pick up my phone and type out a quick text to Rob, Maddie's brother-in-law, so she isn't bothered with picking me up. I asked if he might be able to pick me up if I sent him my flight information.

Rob responds almost immediately:

> Rob: You bet! Madds is going to be so happy to see you, and she could use a moment of happiness.
>
> Me: Great, I appreciate you. Let's keep this a surprise.
>
> Rob: You got it!

I hope he's right about her being happy to see me because the last thing I would want to do is cause her more stress.

My grandparents and I finished our meal, and I excused myself so I could get things taken care of with my flight and the shop and start packing. Once I had everything done, I sent one final text to Grandad about the time he needed to pick me up.

Then I get settled in bed and go to sleep, dreaming of holding Maddie in my arms again.

• • •

Maddie

My family, Connor, and I decided to go to the cafeteria and eat a meal together. It's late, but we're all hungry, and Mama insisted we all needed a break from the family waiting room area. This gave us a little reprieve from constant thoughts of Jake's prognosis. Of course, Mama was right, as usual.

While we're eating, I glance at my phone and realize I missed a call from Ryder. I pick it up and read the missed call message again. The level of disappointment I feel makes me realize again just how much I miss him.

My parents are now leading the pack as we walk back to the waiting room; Connor and I are close behind them, with Rob and Caroline a few feet behind us.

"So, tell me about this town in California you've been living in?" Connor asks.

I look over at him and try to read his face. There's something in his tone, but I push it aside because I remind myself we're friends now. We're moving forward into a new era of Connor and Madelyn. It's one of friendship and appreciation for what once was; it was the keyword in all of this.

"It's beautiful and quaint, and honestly, I love it. I love

the bed and breakfast I work at, the people in the town, and the nature that surrounds it. I never saw myself living anywhere but in Texas until now."

"Sounds amazing. Almost storybook-like. Does this mean you're going back?"

I pick at my nails like I always do when I'm nervous and divided about a decision.

"Well, I do love it. I like the life I've made there. It's hard to imagine not returning because I would be leaving a lot behind."

"You'd be leaving a lot here, too."

My head snaps in his direction. I wanted to yell and maybe even tell him to mind his own damn business, but I decided against it. Instead, I simply reply, "Yeah, I would."

We walk a little further in silence. Then, suddenly, an arm slings over my shoulder, and Caroline is beside me. "Can we chat a minute?"

I look over at her, a bit startled, but I can see she is eyeing Connor. He notices, too, and says, "I'll catch up with your parents." Caroline and I nod.

"Where's Rob?" I ask.

"Oh, he stopped in the bathroom." She tells me, then pauses for only a split second. "Madds, why is Connor still here?"

I stop in my tracks and swing my head in her direction. "Caro, it's fine. He's been a part of our family practically our whole lives."

"Yeah, and he broke up with you. He said he didn't want a future with you, which in my book says he also no longer wanted to be a part of our family."

"He apologized, Caro. He regrets how he handled things, and I'm over it. Plus, I don't have the energy to fight Connor with everything we have going on."

"You're too good, Madelyn. Do you know that?"

"No, I'm not."

"Fine, what about Ryder?"

"What about him?"

"Is he the reason you're over this thing with Connor?"

"Maybe. But I also think I just realized that my life was meant to be so much more."

"With Ryder? Did you ever tell him how you felt?"

"I don't know, and no, you called about Jake before I had the chance."

Caroline throws her hands in the air, making sounds of frustration.

"Look, Caro. I do have feelings for Ryder. I miss him. He is everything I never realized I was missing. But then this happened, and I realized I needed to be with my family. So, do I have feelings for Ryder? Yes, I do. So many feelings. Strong, all-encompassing feelings, but I would never forgive myself if I hurt him. And I can't promise him I can live in Cambria. I can't ask him to leave here either because his grandparents are his world. His family."

"Neither of you can live your lives for your families. We don't expect you to, and I'd put money on the fact that neither does his family. It's wrong of you not even to give him the option to choose you."

"Caroline, I can't think of myself right now. All I can think of is Jake and what is happening with him right now."

Caro places her arm around my shoulder again. She

squeezes and says, "Fine, but promise me you'll stop giving up your happiness for other people."

I lean my head on her shoulder as we walk. "I love you,
Caro."

"I love you, too."

CHAPTER 31

Ryder

I follow Rob through the hospital. He picked me up about forty minutes ago, and although this was the first time we'd met, it felt like I'd known him for years. He's funny and down to earth. Not to mention, I can feel the love he has for the entire Jennings family.

"I'm sure they're all in the family waiting room together. It's pretty cool; they have these rooms for individual families that need to stay at the hospital for an extended period of time. It even has a shower. I haven't been able to get any of them to leave this place the entire six days."

"I don't know the rest of them, but I've come to know Maddie quite well, and nothing about that surprises me. She had to get it from somewhere."

"Oh, yeah. It's amazing how one family can be so alike. They're all pretty amazing."

I smile at the thought. Because if Maddie's family is half as unique as she is, then they must be something special.

"She's going to be happy to see you, man. You coming here when you don't know any of us…that means something."

"I hope so."

"Here we are," Rob says as he opens the door to the family waiting room.

Rob walks in first while I hang back in the hallway, and I hear a couple of people say hello to him. I slowly enter through the doorway, and when I do, Rob is facing me. Next to him is a petite brunette, who I can only assume is Caroline, Maddie's sister. She gives me a wide grin. I glance around the room and see Maddie. She's sitting in a chair in a conversation with a blonde guy. He's sitting close to her, and he's touching her wrist. They're both studying something they must find funny because they both start to laugh.

At that exact moment, she lifts her head and sees me.

Her laugh falters, and she stands, her mouth hanging slightly open. The guy sitting next to her is startled by her abrupt change in position. He is watching her and not looking in my direction until her eyes settle on me.

She takes a few steps toward me, her hand covers her mouth, and she lets out a small sob. "Oh my God, Ryder!"

The guy is now forgotten; I can only see her as she rushes toward me. Taking several steps to meet her, I reach her, and she throws her arms around me. I return her embrace. She pushes me back, looks at me with a huge grin, then hugs me again. "Hey, gorgeous."

She pushes back again and looks at me, tears hanging

on the edge of her lashes.

"How? I…I don't understand."

"Well, how is it? I got on a plane this morning. I texted Rob when I made the decision I needed to come here, and he picked me up. I told him to keep it a secret. I was going to ask you, but you didn't answer when I called, so I just made the decision to come. I hope it's okay?"

"God, yes. It's perfect. Amazing." She hugs me again. "Thank you."

Someone clears their throat from behind me, so I turn, and I see Maddie light up.

"Mama…Daddy, this is Ryder Evans. Ryder, these are my parents, John and Maryanne Jennings."

I reach out and shake each of their hands. Maryanne pulls me into a hug. I can see now that Maddie gets her beautiful auburn hair from her mother. "Nice to meet you both. Maddie has told me so much about you both. Your whole family. I'm sorry to be meeting you under these circumstances." Maryanne Jennings hugs me again.

"No need to apologize. Madelyn has told us about you. Thank you for taking care of her."

"I'm not sure I'm taking care of her, ma'am. She can pretty much handle herself."

Suddenly, two small arms are wrapped around my shoulders. "Hi! I'm Madds' sister, Caroline." When she pulls back, I can see now that Maddie and her sister are practically identical, with the exception of their hair color and stature. Caroline is nearly as tall but has a slightly smaller frame.

"Hi, nice to finally meet you in person rather than just

sharing some random two-word sentences over speaker-phone."

Everyone is exactly how I imagined them. Warm and welcoming. Maddie is standing next to me, her eyes bouncing between all of us, amusement on her face. Something I haven't seen in a while. I missed her while she was here.

All of a sudden, I feel someone standing close behind us. I turned and saw the blonde guy who had been talking to Maddie when I had first walked. He's standing directly behind me. He is tall and lanky. There's something about the way he's eyeing me up and down that makes me feel like he's sizing me up. It's an unwelcome feeling, unlike what I feel from the rest of the Jennings crew.

Suddenly, Maddie is standing between us, looking at both of us with wide eyes and an awkward smile on her face.

"Uh, Ryder, this is…uh…Connor Anderson. Connor, this is my...friend, Ryder Evans."

Shit, this is Connor. Friend, is that what I am? We both stare at each other. I quickly snap to attention, realizing everyone in the room is watching us in anticipation. I stick my hand out in a friendly gesture, although I'm feeling anything but friendly. I'm actually feeling sick. Connor hesitates, looking at my hand for a moment before deciding to accept the gesture.

"Nice to meet you," we both say at the same time.

We drop our handshake almost as quickly as it started. Now is not the time. My mind keeps focusing on the fact that Maddie introduced me as her friend. If I were in the right frame of mind, not jet-lagged and definitely not caught off guard, then I would realize we never defined what we are, so what else would she say? It's not like she was going to introduce me as her lover or the guy she's been sleeping with nearly daily for the past six months.

Nope, now is not the time. This is about supporting her during this situation with her brother, who is still in a coma. Who is still on life support. That is what is important. Not the person standing across from me who broke her heart in a million pieces and sent her halfway across the country. Not the guy who she thought was the love of her life for nearly half of her existence.

"Ryder…"

I hear Maddie's voice, and it seems so far away.

"Ryder?"

I look over at her, and she seems nervous.

"Oh, yeah, I'm sorry. I must be tired from traveling."

"Uh, yeah, I was wondering if you want to take a walk and get something to eat or drink. We can talk."

When I look around the room again, everyone has spread out and settled into other things. Mr. and Mrs. Jennings are sitting huddled together, looking at something on an iPad. Rob and Caroline are calling their kids on Facetime so Caroline can talk to them. And Connor, he's sitting back in the same seat he was in when I showed up. His head is bent down, resting in his hands with his elbows on his knees.

I look back at Maddie, and she is still watching me expectantly. "Sure, I could use something to drink."

Together, we leave the room silently and walk down the hall. In fact, I follow Maddie. Neither of us says a word until we're sitting across from one another at a table in the corner, away from everyone else in the cafeteria.

Maddie is the first to break the silence. "I'm so sorry. I know that was awkward. I should've told you at some point that Connor has been here with my family. It's nothing."

"It's fine. Are you back together?"

"No, it's nothing like that at all. He's just always been a part of my family, and he was trying to be supportive."

"Okay. Tell me about your brother."

She regards me for a moment, completely silent. It's like she wanted to say more about Connor and her family and maybe something else, but she decides against it.

"There still hasn't been any change other than the swelling is subsiding. The doctor did say this is positive, but he still hasn't woken up, and we won't know if there is any permanent damage until he does. If he does."

"He will," I say, covering her hand with mine.

"I have to believe he will."

"Then believe it."

She rests her other hand on top of mine and begins to stroke it with her thumb. It's a light, gentle touch. It brings up a memory of lying next to her in bed early one morning and how, this particular morning, she was touching and kissing me all over. It was like she was worshiping me in a way a person would do if they were savoring the taste of something that might disappear before they were satisfied.

"I've missed you," she says, her eyes concentrating on our joined hands.

"I've missed you, too, Maddie. I hope you're not upset

that I just showed up here. I know I'm a stranger in a time that is so personal for your family."

Her eyes snap up to mine. "You are not a stranger, Ryder Evans."

I want to ask her: Then what am I? But then I remember I'm her friend. And that is true. We are friends, and that is what she needs right now. Even if I want to give her everything this life has to offer, I will wait and hope that the time comes for me to let her know. I hope that I'm not too late.

CHAPTER 32

Maddie

Ryder has been in Texas for three days. Jake has been unconscious for nine days. My family hadn't left the hospital until the day Ryder got to town. He convinced me that night that I needed to go home and get some real sleep.

My family had a powwow and decided he was right. We would start taking turns. My mama insisted she wasn't leaving, so we all ensured we cared for her. Either my dad, Caro, or I stayed with her.

Connor continued to come and go and always forced himself into all conversations. Ryder seems to accept his presence, which didn't surprise me. Connor only seems to be annoyed by Ryder's kindness. My family appears oblivious to all of the tension.

For me, it's still uncomfortable.

Connor has been touchier. Ryder has been more distant with regard to intimacy. All that matters right now is that he is here. Once we get some answers about Jake, then I will be able to think. For now, I'm just trying to hold myself together for me and my family. It's quiet right now because everyone is doing their own thing. My dad, Rob, and Ryder are all on their phones. Connor hasn't shown up yet today. I feel something in the air and can't put my finger on it, making me uneasy.

"Hey there." Ryder's voice pulls me from my thoughts.

"Hey," I smile as best I can. I'm feeling wearier than I have in days.

"I'm heading to the cafeteria with your dad and Rob. Caroline is asleep on the cot. Your mom is still in with Jake. Do you want to come with us and walk for a bit?"

All I can think about when I look at him is how wonderful he is. And I'm struck by the fact that I have decisions to make. I don't know how I can make them.

"Maddie?"

"Oh, yeah, no. I think I'll stay here. Could you bring me some hot tea?"

"Of course. I'll be back soon."

He leans forward and places a soft peck on my cheek.

I watch as Ryder leaves with my dad and Rob. I love how they're all getting along.

The silence is almost deafening, which allows my mind to drift again. I've changed over the last seven months. I feel stronger. Happier. And more independent. And so much of that is because of Ryder.

I also miss my family, and they need me. I need them. Especially now, even if Jake wakes up, his recovery will be extensive. How could I selfishly leave them all again?

To find me? I don't know if I can, which breaks my heart.

I hear the door open, and looking up, I see Connor walking into the room.

"Hey, Maddie, how's it going today?"

"Hey, same as all the other days," I tell him. He walks over and takes a seat next to me.

Glancing around the room, Connor asks, "Where is everyone?"

"Oh, Caro is asleep on the cot. Mama is with Jake. And Daddy, Rob, and Ryder went to the cafeteria."

"I see. Well, I was hoping to talk to you alone for a minute anyway, so this seems like the perfect opportunity."

"Oh, alone?" I question. I stand up and pace the room. I can't keep sitting, but I'm exhausted. I am exhausted by the waiting and all the little things life keeps throwing my way. Not to mention my feelings of uncertainty. Connor makes it worse in some ways because he clouds all my thoughts. I can't imagine what he has to say, but I find that I don't care to hear it. Mainly because I think I've heard enough from him. I'm trying to hear myself for once. Of course, I'm going to listen, though.

He stands and walks up to me until he is directly in front of me. "Maddie, I don't know what is happening with that Ryder guy. But I need to say some things before I miss the opportunity. I had planned on waiting until we knew what was happening with Jake, but…"

I put my hand up. "Stop, Connor. What are you doing?" Please, not now. Why now, I want to scream.

"Maddie, hear me out. Please."

I take a deep breath. That's the first time in a long time

that Connor sounded like the boy I fell in love with all those years ago. I give him a nod to say what he needs to say.

"I can't let someone come in and take you away from me. I still love you, Maddie."

"My God, Connor. You've got to be kidding me. Why now?"

"I know this may not be the ideal time or place to tell you all of this, but as I said, I feel like I have no other choice."

"You left me. You broke it off with me and broke my heart. And now you what? Want me back?"

"I lost my way. I got confused and forgot about all the important things."

"Yes, you did. But you can't expect me to throw my arms around you and take you back because you've finally decided we had something special."

"I love you, Madelyn. I always have, and I always will. You're the only girl, now woman, I've ever loved."

There was a time when these were the exact words I wanted to hear from Connor Anderson. I had wished and hoped he would come to his senses and see what he was throwing away. But that was before before Cambria. Before I knew it, I didn't need a man to be worthy. Before, I found a man who made me feel like I didn't need to do anything but be the person I was by simply existing. And yet, I loved Connor most of my life. I don't want to hurt him, even if he hurt me. He has so many of my firsts. I will always be thankful for the life we had together. The childhood we shared. Our teenage years. And even those early adult moments that guided us to where we are today. I will always love Connor. But now I know that loving someone doesn't mean you are meant to be together. Love doesn't have to mean forever.

"Say something," he pleads.

"Connor, I do love you. I will always love you. You will always be the first boy I fell in love with—my first kiss. The first person to love me back. So, yes, I love you and always will." A wide grin spreads across his face, and I take no satisfaction in the fact that this tells me he's not prepared for my "but." Before I finished, I hugged him, and he hugged me back. It's so familiar, yet it doesn't feel the same. It's not my safe place anymore. It no longer feels like home. I pull back from our hug.

"Maddie, you don't know…"

"Connor, I wasn't finished. I mean it when I say I love you and always will, but I'm not in love with you anymore. I realize now that you were right. We were so consumed by our love that we forgot to grow up together. That isn't healthy, and it isn't real grown-up love. You will always be special to me."

His smile falters. He looks heartbroken, and that hurts me. It's not what I wanted, but I had to be honest.

"I'm sorry," I whisper.

He squares his shoulders and looks me dead in the eye. "Don't be. I'm sorry. I hope you know this wasn't the only reason I've been hanging around. I do love your family like my own. I love Jake, and I'm worried sick. I guess I just hoped…"

Connor doesn't finish because my dad and Rob walk

232

through the door.

"Hey, Connor," my dad says.

Clearing his throat, Connor replies, "Hey, Mr. Jennings. Rob."

"Connor."

I keep expecting Ryder to come through the door with them. "Where's Ryder? Wasn't he with y'all?"

"What? He isn't back yet?" my dad asks.

"Yeah, he said he wanted to get your tea and left about five minutes before we did."

"Huh, I wonder where he is. Maybe I'll go look for him," I say.

Caro walks out of the small extra room where she is napping on the cot.

"What's going on?" she asks.

"I'm not sure where Ryder..." I start before I'm interrupted.

"He's awake! Jake is awake! The doctors are checking him out now!" Mama rushes through the door, a smile on her face and tears running down her cheeks.

A collective gasp sounds through the room. We all hug and cry happy tears.

Ryder. Where is he? I need to find him to tell him Jake has woken up.

CHAPTER 33

Ryder

She still loves him. If I was ever unsure, I'm sure now. I heard it loud and clear from her own mouth. *"Connor, I do love you. I will always love you. You will always be the first boy I fell in love with—my first kiss. The first person to love me back. So, yes, I love you and always will."*

Hearing Maddie say those words was like a dagger to my heart. I feel crushed. I'm sick to my stomach. How did I let myself fall so hard for someone who doesn't even love me back?

As soon as I heard these words, I couldn't listen any longer. Now, I'm wandering aimlessly through the corridors of the hospital. Her tea is still in my hand. I toss it into the trash as I pass it.

"Oh my God, Ryder! There you are! You will never believe it!" Maddie suddenly appears down the hall; she's running toward me. "Ryder! Jake is awake. He...he woke up!"

She practically jumps into my arms when she reaches me, and I can't do anything but catch her. I hear what she's saying, but all I can think is—*but you still love him.*

"Did you hear me?" she asks, looking at me with confusion as I set her back down on her feet.

Did I hear her when she said she loved him and always would? Yes, and it ripped my heart from my chest.

"Ryder?"

Good lord, I need to get a grip. This still isn't about me. About us. About an *"us,"* I guess that never was. I shake it off and push it deep down.

"Yeah...yeah, I heard you. I guess I'm just in shock. This is fantastic!"

A look of concern passes over her features.

"Are you okay?"

"Yes, we should get back to your family."

"Yes, Mama said the doctors are checking him over and will let us know how things look once they're done." She takes my hand in hers; it's soft and warm. I don't want to let go. "Where did you go anyway? Dad and Rob said they thought you would've beat them back to the room."

"I got lost," I lie to her for the first time. She doesn't need to know I heard her. She doesn't need to know that I thought we were more than friends even after she introduced me as her friend.

She laughs, and it's the first truly genuine laugh I've heard from her since we were in Cambria together. "Lost? My word...hey, where's my tea?"

"I dropped it. I'm sorry." The second lie.

"Oh, no big deal. I don't need it anymore."

Maddie loops her arm through mine. Together, we walk back to the family waiting room. She is full of chatter and excitement. Life has been breathed back into her. A lively Madelyn Jennings is a force to be around. I can't help but wonder if it's her brother or the confessions of love that have her so happy.

. . .

Maddie

There's something wrong with Ryder. I can't figure out what it could be. From the moment I found him alone in the hallway, he's been off. Distant. And when I thought I could ask him what the next step was with me, with us, Ryder seemed to be somewhere else.

I walk into my room and find him packing his things into his suitcase. My stomach drops.

"What are you doing?"

"I'm packing, Maddie. I was here to support you while Jake was still critical. Because that is what friends do. But I need to get back. To my family. To the shop."

Tears threaten to spill over. "You're leaving already?"

He looks up at me. There's pain in his eyes. I can see it resting there, covering his beautiful pale green eyes. "You don't need me anymore. You have your family. Connor."

Then, it all starts to come together like a puzzle. The pieces lock together into one. He heard my conversation with Connor. Or at least part of it. He's pushing me away.

"Ryder, I do need you."

His hands stop mid-fold on his shirt, and he looks up at me.

"Madelyn, you don't, and that's okay. You don't need a friend now. You need your family."

I hate the way he just said my name. I wouldn't say I like the way he said the word friend even more. So formal and with such indifference. He heard something. Except he has it all wrong. How do I make him listen?

"Ryder, whatever you're thinking...you're wrong."

"You don't know what I'm thinking, Madelyn."

"Maddie."

"What?"

"Quit calling me Madelyn. You don't call me Madelyn. You call me Maddie. Or baby. Or gorgeous, but not Madelyn. So, stop. Stop all of this and listen to me."

He throws the folded shirt in his bag and zips it up. I can feel his frustration, anger, and hurt growing and pouring out. It's almost suffocating.

"Listen to me."

"I can't."

I suck in a breath like I can't find air because the agony I hear in his voice just cuts me.

"Why? Tell me why?"

His back is to me. I want to turn him around so we can look into one another's eyes, but I'm afraid I won't survive what I see.

"I can't stand to hear you tell me that you love someone else. For me, these last six months haven't just been sex and me passing time. I can't hear you call me your friend again."

The tears are no longer threatening to make an appearance. They're showing themselves in full force.

"Ryder, you don't understand what you heard."

"What I heard?"

"Yes, I've only just realized you heard me talking to Connor this morning."

I wipe the tears away and wait for him to confirm what I already know.

"There is no way to misunderstand what I heard, Maddie."

"But there is. Because you only heard part of it. You didn't hear everything."

He finally turns to face me again. I can't tell if he's angry or hurt. Like I'm lying to him.

"Explain then. Explain how I misunderstood when I heard you tell Connor that you love him. You always have, and you always will."

"Because while I said all that and meant it, I also said that I wasn't in love with him anymore, and I realized we weren't meant to be. I told him that two people can love one another but that love doesn't always mean forever."

Ryder sits on the edge of my bed. His head down.

"What are you saying?" he finally asks.

"I've been too afraid to define us because I've worried I won't be enough for you. I worried you'd get tired of me."

I kneel in front of him and take his hands in mine. He looks down into my eyes.

"I've fallen in love with you, Ryder."

He slides down onto his knees in front of me. He takes my face and cups his hands around it.

"I've fallen in love with you, too, Maddie."

His lips cover mine in a slow, sensual kiss. He takes his time, creating that tingling sensation he is so good at igniting. We kiss like we will never need air again.

When we finally stop, I say, "Please stay. Stay with me."

"I can't. I should go back tomorrow. But, when things are settled with Jake, come home to me."

And this is where I break our hearts all over again. I can't make that promise to him or myself. He sees it in my eyes before I even say it.

"I can't make that promise. I want to so badly, but I... my family. They need me, and I don't know where that leaves ...us. It's the reason I hesitated to tell you how I felt for so long."

He nods, then stands. Grabbing his bag, he starts toward the door.

"And I can't wait around to see if you're going to break my heart anymore."

He disappears out of the door and out of the house. I sit on the floor with tears flowing and in pain, with no one to blame but myself. I just broke my own heart. This time, I wonder if I can put it back together.

CHAPTER 34

Maddie

I thought not seeing Ryder for five days was hard. But two weeks without seeing or talking to him has been nearly unbearable.

Since he left, I've kept myself busy. Visiting Jake in the hospital. Spending time with Caro, Rob, and the kids. Hanging out in the evenings with my parents at home. No one has asked me why Ryder left so abruptly.

In true Ryder fashion, he put his hurt aside and made sure he said his goodbyes. He left me out as one of his reasons for leaving and explained he had to get back to his shop.

But I can see the way they all look at me. Full of pity. Even Caro has kept her comments and opinions to herself.

I've tried texting and calling him in hopes of finding out how he's doing. To see if he's hurting as badly as I am, but I realize I don't really have the right because I'm the reason for my hurt. He hasn't returned any of them. Call or text. I've spoken to Henry, Evelyn, and even Rosalind. They all act as sweet as ever and tell me how much they miss me. They never ask when I'm coming back, even though I can hear it in their voices that they want to ask.

I walk into my parents' house, and it's quiet.

As I make my way to my room, I scream when I hear someone say my name.

"Madelyn?"

"Daddy! You scared the bejeezus out of me!"

"Well, this is my house. I'm sorry I didn't announce myself."

I laugh and walk around the couch, taking a seat.

"Yes, it is your house."

My dad studies me for a minute.

"What are you doing, Madelyn?"

"Well, I thought I would sit here and hang out with you."

"That's not what I meant. I mean, what are you still doing here?"

I stare at him, my mouth hanging open in surprise.

"What do you mean? I'm helping my family."

My dad gets out of his chair and walks to the couch, sitting beside me.

"Maddie, we appreciate it, too. But you have your own life to live. Your family will be fine. We love you and want to see you happy. And you're not happy."

"I am happy. I'm with all the people I love and who love me."

"Are you though?"

I stand up and pace the room like I always do when my

anxiety starts to come alive.

"I don't know what you mean?"

"Sure you do, sweetheart. You love that man. You've never looked at anyone the way you looked at him. And even better, I've never seen anyone look at you the way he did. He sees you the way I see your mother. I mean, he flew to another state because you needed him. So, I will ask you again: what are you doing?"

Taking a seat on the couch again, I look at my dad. My daddy. My hero. And I hug him as tightly as I can. "I'm scared, Daddy. I was scared he would leave me. Scared that if I live my own life, it might hurt all of you somehow."

"That would never happen. As a parent, my whole life was spent praying you would grow up and live your own life. Find love and create a family of your own. You find that life will never hurt me. Or your mother. If you throw it all away because you're afraid, it will hurt us."

"What if it's too late?"

"I don't think you're that easy to get over. But you won't know unless you go there and allow yourself to be vulnerable. You deserve this chance, and so does Ryder."

"I love you so much, Daddy. Thank you for being such a good dad."

"I love you, too, Madelyn. And it's easy to be a good dad when you have good kids."

• • •

Ryder

Maddie has called and texted me multiple times a day since I left Texas two weeks ago. Yes, I'm being stubborn because I haven't responded to one of them. But it hurts too much. I hit decline whenever I see her name pop up on my screen. It's too painful. I'm not ready to hear her voice, especially if she is going to tell me she still can't choose me.

I'm sitting across from Gran and Grandad having Sunday dinner. Rosalind sits next to me, chatting about school.

My phone vibrates, and I pull it out and glance at it. Usually, I try to respect my grandparents' rule of no phones at the table, but Billy is closing up tonight, and I like to keep my phone on, just in case.

But it isn't Billy. It's her. I hit decline.

"Is that Madelyn?" Grandad asks. Everyone looks at him, including me, but he ignores us. "You need to just talk to her, Ry," he continues.

"Henry, stay out of it," Gran says.

"No, he has been moping around for two weeks."

"I have not been moping," I say.

"You have," Ros chimes in.

"Stay out of it," I tell her.

"I only speak the truth," she ignores me.

"Would you all just mind your own business?"

Now, I'm getting angry. I'm angry because they're butting into my business. Angry because Maddie said she couldn't choose me. Furious because they're right. I have been moping.

"Ryder, we're just worried about you. And about Maddie. She doesn't sound like herself. She sounds sad and tired."

"You've spoken to her?"

"Well, yeah, duh, we all have. You aren't the only person who had a relationship with Maddie," Ros snarks.

My family has been talking to her. They've heard her voice. Does she sound sad? It doesn't matter. I knew she was sad when I left her parents that night. But what I wouldn't give to hear her voice again. To hear her say she loves me again.

But I can't take that chance. I can't feel that pain of rejection from her again. I won't survive. I have to ask them.

"Has she said if and when she is coming back to Cambria?"

They all look at me as if I asked a forbidden question.

"We haven't asked her. Maybe if you would answer her phone calls or texts, you could ask her yourself," Gran says, with a slight harshness she's never used with me before.

I cringe at her tone. It sounds like even Gran is upset by how she spoke to me, but she won't apologize because we both know I deserve it.

I can't say I will answer next time she calls, but I can say I miss her like crazy.

CHAPTER 35

Maddie

Pulling into the town of Cambria this time was completely different from when I first arrived. For one, I'm in a rental car, and it isn't about to break down. But, most importantly, this time, I'm driving past the population sign, knowing exactly who I am as a woman instead of searching for her.

The one similar thing is I'm still in awe of this quaint little town and all its charm.

My mission is different. This time, I'm here to mend more than just my broken heart. I'm here for love. And I'm here to take a chance on a new forever that is unknown but full of possibilities.

Driving onto Main Street, I see Ryder's shop in the distance. His truck is parked out back, just as I hoped. He's either at home or in the shop. I pull around to the back and park next to him.

I tried his apartment first, and when there was no answer, I decided to head around to the shop.

I stop, my heart pounding in my chest, just before I come to the garage entrance. *Be brave, Madelyn. He said he loves you. You're the one who didn't choose him right away. So, get a grip and take a chance,* I tell myself.

Taking another breath, I take another step forward until I'm at the garage's opening. Music is playing loudly, so I try yelling when I finally decide to speak.

"Hello!"

Nothing. That's when I spot the bell on the wall, so I walk over and press it. It buzzes, and I yell out, "Hello!"

I heard a voice from beneath the truck resting on the lift.

"Yeah, I will be right there."

It's him. Hearing his voice again causes me to shake. I think about running, and I take one step toward the door so that when he walks up, my back is turned.

"How can I help…" his voice drifts off. "Maddie?"

I close my eyes and release a breath before I turn around.

"Hey, Ryder," I say as I face him.

"What are you doing here?"

"I tried calling to tell you, but you didn't answer. So, I came anyway." I put my arms out and up in the air. "Surprise."

"But what are you doing here?" he asks again.

Without thinking or answering his question, I ask him, "What do you think real love is?"

"Excuse me?"

"Well, I've been thinking about this a lot over the last

few weeks. And I'm wondering what your opinion is. What do you think real love is?"

He thinks for a minute, his hands resting on his hips. Oil smudges on his shirt and cheek. He's never been sexier.

"Well, I think it's when someone loves you so totally and completely for the person you are and not the person they want you to be."

"See, that's the same answer I came up with." He stares at me, seemingly confused by where this conversation is going. "Henry asked me a funny question when I called yesterday. But this was after my dad asked me a different question. He confused me at first." I ramble. And I know I'm not making a lick of sense, but I don't care. I have a point. Ryder stares at me in confusion. "Ask me what the questions were, Ryder."

He seems a little reluctant, but I think he can tell that I won't give up, and if he's going to find out why I'm here, he will have to follow my lead.

"What question did your dad ask, Maddie?"

"He asked me what I was doing."

Ryder stares at me, his face showing his perplexity.

"I told him I was hanging out with him. And he told me that wasn't what he meant. He wanted to know why I was there…in Texas with all of them. When you and my heart were here in Cambria."

"I told him I was scared, Ryder. Have you ever been so scared that you made a mistake?"

"I'm scared now," he says.

"But will you make a mistake like I did? Because I did. I probably made the biggest mistake of my life. Because

I let the person I love think that I didn't love him enough, and that's where Henry's question comes into play."

"Maddie, I…"

I step toward him and put my hand up to stop him from talking.

"Do you know what Henry asked me when I called to say I was coming to Cambria?"

Ryder shakes his head.

"He said, 'Maddie, dear, is Ryder the one? Is he the one you would give up your last breath for?'"

Ryder doesn't blink. It's like my story finally caught his attention, and he can't turn away because he might miss something.

"Ryder, I wasn't afraid of those questions. Those were easy because they were about my feelings, and those are the ones I'm most sure about. I've been sure about the answer to those questions for a long time."

He takes a step toward me. "What are your answers to those questions? The ones you aren't afraid of and are so sure about."

"I told Henry that yes, without a doubt, you're the one. The one that is a real love. The one I would give up everything familiar for. The one I would give up my last breath for. Now, I have a question for you."

"Just one?" he asks, a smile playing on his lips.

"No, two. Am I the one, Ryder? Am I the one you'd give up your last breath for?"

Closing the last bit of distance, our mouths mere inches apart, Ryder says, "You're the real kind of love. The one. And every breath I've taken since I met you has been for you, and every one till my last will be for you."

He catches a tear that escapes down my cheek. "I love you, Maddie."

"I will never be scared again. I love you, Ryder."

Then we kiss. We kiss like it's our first. Our last. Our forever.

THE END.

ABOUT THE AUTHOR

Shirl Rickman is a storyteller. A wife. A mother. A believer. She spends her days in a chaotic pursuit of happiness. There isn't anything she loves more than her husband and kids, but if she had to choose a close runner-up it would be coffee and laughing.

Shirl and her husband are spending their empty nester days working hard and traveling as often as possible.

Website
www.shirlrickmanauthor.com

Facebook
https://www.facebook.com/shirlrickmanauthor

Facebook Reader Group
www.facebook.com/rickmanreaders

Instagram
https://www.instagram.com/shirlrickmanauthor

Twitter
https://www.twitter.com/shirl_rickman